EMBRACE THE DARK

EMBRACE THE DARK

Caris Roane

Copyright © 2012 by Caris Roane

Formatting and cover by Bella Media Management.

ISBN: 978-1477582916

THE BLOOD ROSE SERIES
BOOK ONE

EMBRACE THE DARK

CARIS ROANE

Dear Reader

EMBRACE THE DARK is here at last: Novella #1 of the Blood Rose Novella Series!

Many of you know me from my Guardians of Ascension series, published by St. Martin's Press, beginning in January of 2011 with ASCENSION.

For some time now, I've wanted to write a novella series to help fill in the months between the releases of my full-length novels. Because I have a long-standing love affair with vampires, I decided to continue with my favorite fanged creatures and to that end created my Blood Rose Novella Series. This time, however, I added several different species to a world I've called the Nine Realms of North America.

Of course, vampires still end up on top!

Governing each realm is a 'mastyr' vampire, an uber-powerful vampire with sufficient preternatural ability to defeat the long-standing enemy of realm-folk: the deadly Invictus wraith-pairs.

Our beleaguered mastyr vampires also suffer from chronic blood starvation and can only be sated by a phenomenon called *a blood rose*.

Each realm exists in a parallel plane to a major city in North America and the first novella, **EMBRACE THE DARK**, takes us to Flagstaff, Arizona where my hero and heroine cross paths.

I hope you enjoy this new take on paranormal lore.

EMBRACE THE DARK is a novella of 45,000 words, which is an approximate paperback length of 135 pages.

For more information about the series, visit me at: www.CarisRoane.com

For lots of Facebook fun, you can find me posting frequently on my wall. I also encourage my fans to post, so there's lots of sharing of music and pics of all kinds. Facebook search: *Caris Roane*

Prior to writing sensual paranormal romance, I wrote *sweet* Regency Romance for Kensington Publishing Corp., and was fortunate to publish almost 50 Regency novels and novellas during that time under the pseudonym, Valerie King. In 2005, Romantic Times Magazine honored me with a Career Achievement Award in Regency Romance. You can learn more about my Regency work at: ValerieKing-romance.com.

I've been blessed to write romance all these years.

I hope you enjoy, **EMBRACE THE DARK**!

Blessings,
Caris Roane

Chapter One

Mastyr Vampire Gerrod, of Merhaine Realm, lifted a hand toward the human, Abigail, then let it fall away. She stood with her back to him, ignoring him, delighting in the wedding festivities, laughing often.

Sweet Goddess, even her laughter spiked his blood-need, which caused other needs to rise as well. His desire for her was never far away and deepened now, echoing through each cell of his vampire body, stiffening muscles and other parts, begging for sustenance, all kinds.

He should have been beyond such madness. He was three-hundred-years-old, for the Goddess's sake. But ever since Abigail Kirkland had made her presence known and felt in Merhaine, he'd been held hostage by even the scent of her.

Like crushed rosemary.

He breathed in, his nostrils flaring. A full sliver of heaven in that delicate scent, with just enough woman beneath to rob him of rational thought.

And she a human.

He flexed his biceps: he was that mad. He had to work not to let his fangs descend, else everything he felt would be on display for even the lesser folk to know and understand. He wouldn't let her humiliate him.

This madness was *maddening*.

He stood behind her, and a little off to her right side. He could almost see her profile. She knew he was there, but she was ignoring him. She had told him that his temper irked her and she wished he would be silent.

He could have her killed for saying such a thing to him, he, the Mastyr Vampire of the Merhaine Realm, one of the Nine Realms of North America. Did she not understand that he ruled this realm?

He should walk away. There were many at the wedding reception expecting his attention, several mayors, council members.

Yet he couldn't do so since apparently his leather boots had rooted to the earth. What power was this she held over him? He had never understood, not in the entire year he'd known her.

As the best man spoke into the mic and delivered a slightly slurred toast to the groom, Gerrod's gaze roved Abigail, his hunger increasing. Her bare shoulders tempted him, called to him, begged for his lips, his fingers, the full length of his tongue. His nostrils flared a little more. Her gown, a soft cream, revealed a portion of her fair back, a large window of skin that set his jaw to trembling. Her long red hair was curled and pulled forward to dangle over her shoulder in beautiful layers over one breast. She had extraordinary eyes, a beautiful light green. He couldn't remember the last time he'd been so taken with a woman.

May the heavens help him. Abigail had teased his mating frequency into a frenzy and he was overwrought. Yet he could do nothing about it. The damn woman was human. He would no more give himself to such a ridiculous creature than he would bring forest gremlins into his bed.

He'd be damned first.

He felt a different frequency resonate, a warning within his mind. Derek's voice telepathed along his Guardsman lane. *We've got signs of Invictus in the southeast.*

Invictus. Not tonight. Damn and hell and back. The enemy was abroad.

Gerrod telepathed. *Are you sure?*

The red wind is blowing.

There were only a handful who could detect the telltale red wind, he and his castle Guard. Several on the Sidhe Council had sufficient power as well as his constant most cherished advisor, Vojalie. Some said the red wind was made of blood that the Invictus sweated when they took to the air. Vampires might have needed blood to live, but the Invictus took blood to sustain their unnatural bonds and didn't care what they left behind, life or death.

Gerrod turned away from Abigail slightly. *Can you contain?* he asked.

I'll need assistance. I've counted eleven in the breach.

The Invictus came from the wastelands in the south, the place they preferred to live once each vile couple invoked the perverted rituals that created their kind. Any combination of realm specie would do, so long as one of the pair was a wraith: Vampire, faerie, elf, troll, shifter, it didn't matter. There were few true wraiths left, those that adhered to simple things like truth and civility, justice and the law. But they were always looked upon with suspicion, which couldn't be helped at this late hour.

The Invictus killed without conscience, without reason and usually in a sadistic manner.

They were a scourge to be feared and to be slaughtered.

Once a wraith took an Invictus mate, the couple was sealed into a symbiotic relationship that tended to break down goodness and give rise to all that was bad. Thievery was preferred to hard work. Killing to the support and nurturing of life. Insular frenzied hedonism to the sacrifices of marriage and family.

When the Invictus took blood, the realm-folk screamed at the draining, no pleasure, all pain. Nor did the Invictus discern, all blood was acceptable. Specie, age, gender, none of it mattered. Just the living, that's all the Invictus needed.

How far away? Gerrod asked. *The wedding is still mid-reception.*

Gerrod's gaze swept in the direction of the bride and groom, a long-awaited fae wedding. They were fair of face, this couple, and toasting each other with bubbling cider. She was already with child, a tradition among the Merhaine faeries. A child was a promise of a blessed union between souls favored by the Goddess. Gillet, the groom, had served on his castle staff for the last century. He had waited a long time for his bride.

Now the Invictus, tonight of all nights. Why? Was there a reason? Had the festivities drawn them? Every media outlet across the realm had made a fuss over the couple. The Hollow County Enquirer had carried a daily piece on every aspect of the couple: The announcement of the forthcoming birth, the betrothal, and wedding preparations.

Even the Invictus would have known of the wedding. Many Merhaine notables were in attendance as well, several city mayors and council members.

Another team member, Jason, telepathed the battle frequency. *The southeastern sector is clear tonight. Gerrod, shall I join Derek?*

Yes, Gerrod pathed. *Rest of the team, report?* A world of pathways and frequencies had tremendous advantages. Long distance communication with those powerful enough to telepath, was a tremendous blessing. All Guards of the Realm could path.

The Invictus were ruthless combatants and never fought with anything resembling decency or honor. A decade ago, Gerrod had lost a valiant vampire Guardsman when an Invictus wraith threw a jug of gasoline on him and set him on fire, laughing all the while.

In the poorer southern regions, drug addicts and prostitutes, even in his realm, often went missing, never to be seen again.

Training had become more rigorous because of the increasing activity. Each Guard now knew to anticipate the unexpected, and training camps had been established for the purpose of evaluating any young vampire, fae, troll, shifter, or elf, who wanted to try for Guard status, male or female. The effort had brought some talent into the castle Guard. Muscle for muscle, however, vampires still had the advantage over other realm-folk so that most Guardsmen were vampires.

One by one, the remaining five Guardsmen gave an all clear for the rest of the realm, at least for now. Yet he felt uneasy. He lifted his chin and issued the orders, *All except Jason, join Derek now. Jason, come to the castle grounds and patrol here but keep a low profile. And Jason, have the head of the patrols get the rest of the*

Guard out tonight, emergency levels.

Done.

His sense of uneasiness grew. At least his men had speed. They could lock onto their traveling frequencies better than all realm-folk. Though Jason was over a hundred miles away, he would arrive in less than twenty minutes. Not half-damn bad.

His gaze never stopped moving over the crowd, or into the forest, or even high into the night sky which was clear, star-studded, and just a circle of dark surrounded by the tips of ponderosa pine trees.

He loved the forest and the dark. Each realm had some manner of forest and dense woodland attached. Vampires needed a place to shelter if caught outside during the day. Tree canopies were necessary to those who had difficulty tolerating sunlight.

Even faeries and elves didn't tolerate sunlight well. The realm world was, for the most part, a world of the night and of the dark.

He shifted his gaze to eye-level and bored his vision deep between the trees, hunting for the peculiar red-wind Invictus sign.

Sweet Goddess, but his land was in trouble, as all the Nine Realms of North America were, if the Invictus engaged in yet another uprising.

At least for now, the wedding party was safe and he could share in the joy of Gillet and his woman.

Abigail chuckled once more, which brought Gerrod's attention sharply back to the woman who had been tormenting him for an entire year. Her laughter glided over his nerves like a fine oil, which simply sent his temper into the top of his head all over again. Why did the human have to be here and why, by all that was worthy in his world, did he have to be drawn to her?

He cast about for the source of her laughter. She looked off to the right so he followed her gaze. One of the trolls had imbibed far too much wedding punch and was listing about. He had already bumped into a few of the guests. Next he jostled a large vampire, who in turn picked him up by the lapels of his lavender silk coat, and glared at the troll face to face. The wedding guests drew a combined gasp.

Vampires were not known for their sweet tempers. Fucking understatement that.

But the troll smiled sloppily and kissed the vampire on the nose. The vampire grimaced, called out a loud growling 'ack', spat off to his left side, but released the troll. The guests breathed again and many chuckled, especially Abigail, as the troll turned and shambled away.

By all the elf-lords, the damned woman laughed too much.

More than anything, he wished he had never heard of Abigail of Flagstaff, a mere human, a bakery owner, the latter being the why of her presence in his realm.

He had opposed the Merhaine Council approving her partnership with an elf to open a bakery in the nearby county of Hollow, one of Merhaine's seven counties. He had believed from the first it was a mistake. However, and this for reasons he could not explain, Abigail was a favorite among realm-folk. She had been providing the sweet-loving trolls, faeries, and elves of his realm with cupcakes—*for all the Nine Realms, cupcakes!*—for well over a year. His castle even had a standing weekly order with her Flagstaff enterprise, a place called *Just Too Sweet!* Yes, with an exclamation point.

And now *he* felt like spitting.

Some of the council were looking to expand into the human world as well, which he believed to be a mistake of enormous proportions. Some of the drugs of the human world had already infected the less prosperous portions of his realm. Didn't his realm have enough trouble managing the constant threat of the Invictus?

And yet, as he sniffed the breeze that flowed over the woman's long red tresses, he could scent rosemary again, and he knew exactly what her skin would taste like beneath his tongue. His body reacted, sharpening, hardening, shuddering, until he was once more grateful for the long leather coat of his Guardsman uniform, and the snug buckled leather pants that held all his absurd firmness well in place.

The woman be damned.

His gaze shifted back to the drunken troll, who now listed sideways and fell into the three-tiered sage-and-honey wedding cake. The fae bride cried out and the groom's cheeks showed an angry wash of red.

The guests, however, began to laugh and Abigail joined them.

He was angry all over again. How dare she laugh?

It was time he took her down a slat or two.

*** *** ***

"You find our customs amusing?"

Abigail turned slightly at the almost growling sound. The words were spoken in a deep low voice, emanating from the vampire Guardsman next to Abigail, the leader of the Merhaine Realm, Mastyr Vampire Gerrod. Of course, he didn't exactly stand next to her. He would never deign to do that. God, forbid, or 'Goddess', as he would say. Instead, he stood slightly behind her, a position of power and control no doubt. She could feel him fuming behind her. Some burr had gotten stuck inside those boots of his.

Abigail turned a little more and glanced up at him. As always, she felt an almost overwhelming attraction to Mastyr Gerrod. He was six-five and though she considered herself tall for a human at five-eleven, still she had to look up, though perhaps not as far this evening since she wore four-inch heels. A very slight advantage against his formidable scowl and heavily muscled body.

The vampire was stunning and ferocious. Because of the books she'd read, she had thought his kind would be pale-skinned from lack of blood, an un-beating heart, and the inability to get a decent tan because of an intolerance for sunlight. But the world of the Realm produced vampires of every possible hue, from the deepest browns and blacks to almost pure white. The solar disability and the persistent blood-needs had nothing to do with skin-tone.

His Guard uniform did not help *at all*. The man looked like a fierce pirate with a soft maroon woven shirt, topped by a thick black calf-length leather coat. The coat wasn't exactly a coat because it didn't have sleeves, just a thick pad of very soft leather at the shoulders that descended in two panels that hung open in the front.

A black leather shoulder strap crossed over his chest, and angled to his waist, undoubtedly a throw-back to times when swords were used. No swords now, just the power that a Guardsman could gather through his battling frequency and send outward through his arms, hands, and chest, tight beams of killing energy. Black leather pants and silver-buckled top boots finished off the uniform that had most women doing double and triple takes.

Gerrod was magnificent, well-built with broad shoulders,

as all the fighting Guardsmen were, his skin an exquisite golden color. He held himself in a proud manner, as befitted his leadership status. Even now his arms were crossed over his chest as he glowered at her.

He had long black hair that flowed away from strong features. His cheeks were pronounced and sharp, his jaw-line angled, his lips full and sensual. But it was his eyes that tore at her, that made his presence almost unbearable. They were the clear blue of a summer mountain sky, so clear that often when she looked at him, she felt as though she was looking back in time and forward all at once.

Of course that he affected her in such a way that she often wanted to simply shed her clothes and fall down on her back, ticked her off. Thank God she was made of sterner stuff, because all these unhelpful reactions strengthened her intention to keep the vampire at bay.

Besides, he was such a pain in the ass, like now. So typical. He'd been standing behind her, *forever*. And when he finally did speak to her, he used that wretched, oh-so-familiar hostile tone of his, this time to challenge her because she'd been laughing.

"You think I'm laughing at your customs?" she returned.

"And what else would you be laughing at, Mistress Abigail?" His words were hard, as they usually were when he spoke to her. She'd at least grown accustomed to that. But because she sensed that he either disliked her or disapproved of her, or both, she simply didn't know why he stayed anywhere near her, like now.

She lifted her chin. "I would never laugh at Merhaine customs. I might disagree with them because I find some to be abhorrent to the status of women in your culture, but I would never laugh."

"I heard you laughing."

She chuckled again but shook her head. She moved back to stand beside him. She wasn't going to continue this conversation staggered as they were, like stair-steps.

"Mastyr Gerrod," she said, lowering her voice. "I found the wedding ceremony, including the way their arms were bound with a vine, charming, poignant, even moving. I laughed just now because a troll fell into a wedding cake. Come on. That was funny."

He grunted his disapproval.

At that, she turned to face him fully. She was exasperated to say the least. "You know, you really need to lighten up."

He glanced down at her. "I have no idea what that means. I have heard the expression time and again, but it makes no sense to me."

"It just means not to take everything so seriously." She waved a hand in the direction of the now smashed wedding cake. "The troll is drunk, that alone is funny. Wouldn't you agree? He's still wobbling around and he has a streak of frosting now between the second and third ridges of his forehead." She glanced over her shoulder then back. "And now his wife is beating him over the head with their son's teddy-shifter-bear. Come on. Even the bride is smiling now and it's her cake that the troll ruined."

Gerrod's lips twitched, and the right side of his lips almost curved creating a faint, lop-sided smile. But that was when she made her mistake. "Yeah, like that. Smile. *Lighten up.*" She poked his arm with two fingers, intent on teasing him a little more.

But the moment she made physical contact with him, the very first ever in her year-long acquaintance with him, something very strange happened. She felt odd waves rolling toward her, waves that felt like fingers gliding over her skin, exploring her, *savoring her.*

She looked up meeting his gaze. Now he turned fully toward her so that they were face to face. Her lips were parted because she was having trouble dragging in air. Why his were, only he could speak to that.

Touching a mastyr vampire wasn't precisely forbidden, but Gerrod had always kept his distance. This was something she'd noticed from the first day she'd met him, that as soon as she was within two feet of him, he stepped away another foot. She had thought it an annoying habit, a sure sign of his continued disapproval. But right now, because she'd touched him, she wasn't so sure.

Abigail's heart began to race. She'd had many concerns about entering into business with an elf partner and opening a bakery deep into Merhaine territory. But right now she realized this was the real danger she faced, that the vampire Mastyr Gerrod, ruler of Merhaine, affected her as though she was always within a hair's breadth of tumbling into bed with him.

She knew the danger the terrible Invictus presented, she even understood that there were factions among the realm-folk who didn't want humans in Merhaine and would do whatever they could to get rid of her *and her kind.* Yes, these things worried her very much. But as she looked into Gerrod's intense blue eyes, she finally understood the true source of every reticence she'd experienced since she'd come to this realm: Dammit, she had the hots for a friggin vampire.

She desired him with a need that seemed to burn through her and touching him just now, brought all that need rushing to the surface yet again.

His gaze shifted from her eyes to her lips and even to her breasts. She could feel the sudden hardening of her nipples as the need spread. How many times had she wondered if he was doing this to her, using vampire powers. But the realm-folk she knew had assured her that vampires, however much the Earth-based myths said otherwise, didn't have the power to enthrall.

The fae population could, but not vampires.

Very strange, this realm world.

So what was this she felt, this deep desire for Gerrod and why, when he looked at her with his eyelids heavy, his lips parted, his nostrils flaring, did she want to take his hand, lead him deep into the forest, and beg him to have his way with her. What was this need?

He stepped closer and though he was frowning heavily like his temper was ready to take off the top of his head, he actually touched her, sliding his hand over her arm. Once again, she felt those strange waves emanating from him and her desire increased almost to a painful stage.

What is that? Her mind cried.

But he leaned close now and stared harder, peering into her eyes. *What did you say?*

She glanced at his lips. They hadn't moved. Telepathy? No, oh, God no. This couldn't be happening, wasn't happening. She knew many in Merhaine could communicate through telepathic frequencies, pathing was what they called it.

Could she?

This couldn't be happening, couldn't be true. She stared into his eyes, horrified, yet she had to know the truth. So, once more she aimed her thoughts carefully, *I wanted to know what I was feeling from your hand. It felt like waves flowing out of you and into me.*

The thought of it, the presence of it, the feel of it beating into her body, brought desire hurtling through her. She planted her hand on his chest. The waves pounded through her now, engulfing her.

He looked so angry and his grip on her arm became painful. *This can't be happening. You can't feel these waves and you can't be reaching me telepathically. It's. Not. Possible.*

Gerrod, what are you doing to me? And please, you are hurting my arm. Vampires were strong.

The pressure diminished but his expression hardened. *You are speaking to me telepathically and you are experiencing my personal frequency, my realm vibration. No one can do that except when I allow it, but you accessed it freely. And you are…human. This cannot not be happening.*

She was struggling to breathe. But his touch, and the flowing waves, had her trapped. She strained toward him, but he kept a grip on her arm, holding her away from him. He squeezed his eyes shut. *This is impossible. You can't be what you seem to be. You can't be. You're human. This is unacceptable.*

Abigail slid her hand up his chest and reached his mouth. She ran her thumb over his lips.

How inappropriate and thank goodness they were standing at the back of the crowd. In the distance, she could hear another groomsman making a toast. Though it was nighttime, the floodlights lit mostly the band, the bridal table, and the dance floor. This far back, she stood in the shadows.

Time came to a swift stumbling halt.

Abigail looked at Gerrod as if for the first time. She felt a call so deep in her soul, driving her toward him, that to not respond, not to say 'yes', felt like a crime for which she would be punished if she didn't obey. She needed this vampire, craved him. For the first time, her vein began to rise in her throat, because that's the only way she could describe what she experienced. She needed him to take her blood because that would complete something essential between them, as essential as the nature of a kiss, as critical as the fulfillment of lovemaking.

Yet, she was human and didn't truly belong in the realm world. She belonged in Flagstaff, the nearest access point to the Merhaine Realm.

The tip of his tongue teased her thumb. *You taste of the sweetest herbs. Dear Goddess, please forgive me.*

Before she knew what he meant by sending that particular message, he took hold of her arm, swung her in the direction of the forest, and led her twenty yards into the dark, a good distance from the crowd that now applauded. Music began at the same time, a lively folk song made for dancing.

He dragged her behind a tree and hauled her into his arms.

She fell against him, limp, her body in full surrender and not caring that this was so inappropriate and doomed to cause all kinds of problems.

For some strange reason as she stared up at him, though the forest was dark, his face was lit in a glow. Vampire magic? He was incredibly beautiful, his black brows thick and arched, his clear blue eyes thickly fringed, his nose straight, his lips full, his cheeks pronounced.

He leaned close, his lips trembling over hers.

"Do I have permission to kiss you?"

God, yes.

"Yes," she whispered, panting against him, her fingers grasping the soft cloth of his loose Guard's shirt. She dug deeper until her fingers found purchase in the hard muscles of his arms. His lips touched hers and the previous waves began to flow, heavier now.

She parted her lips and his tongue entered her, piercing her, plunging in and out.

She connected her hips low and felt the long rope of him. Her knees weakened further.

She suckled his tongue and he groaned again. The waves came faster now and seemed to pluck at every part of her body at once. She wanted to fall on the ground, but in gentle stages he eased back. But by then she was in agony and breathed hard. She pressed her forehead into his shoulder.

What is happening? she asked.

I fear it is something that will alter your life forever, unless you are wise, and choose to leave Merhaine. You would be wise, Abigail, not to come back and I'm begging you to do just that. You are not realm. You don't understand our customs. My people would have great difficulty accepting you.

But beyond that, the Invictus have grown active again. A polite euphemism for death and destruction.

She drew back, but in her heels the uneven ground put her off-balance. She started to fall.

He caught her, righting her, then held her steady.

"Just tell me one thing," she said. "What are the waves that you send through my body. They almost undo me. I…that is…you could have…I wouldn't have objected."

She met his gaze but she was blushing.

A soft strange growl left his lips. So vampires growled at such moments. He wasn't human, but why didn't that seem to matter to her? And why could she speak with him mind to mind? She should have cared, it should have been paramount. And her vein still throbbed, begging for him to take her very life-force.

"I swear you've enthralled me," he said, a deep furrow now between his brows. "This must be your doing, Abigail. It was there from the first."

"Gerrod are you saying that you've been attracted to me since that first day?"

"I won't deny it."

"I thought you disapproved of me."

"I'm frustrated, even distressed, that I'm drawn to you, a very different thing."

She put her finger in the furrow between his brows and rubbed. He let loose with a sigh, closing his eyes. She added, "You're worried all the time."

"Yes." His voice was always little more than a deep, gravelly growl.

"One of the fae told me that there are a million realm in Merhaine. Is this true?"

He nodded.

"You have charge of a million souls then?"

"I do."

"No wonder you rarely laugh." She had meant to tease him but when he didn't even smile, when he looked away from her, she finally understood his most essential self. He was responsible and he put those responsibilities above everything else in his life including his own happiness.

"No wonder your people thrive," she said.

His gaze snapped back to her. "Why do you say that?" Again that deep furrow appeared.

"You've laid your life down for your people, no doubt for decades. Why wouldn't they thrive? But what of you, Gerrod? What of your own happiness?"

He stared down at her with a stunned look in his eye as though she had asked something never heard of before. Then he just looked confused. But as other thoughts intruded, his face hardened. He looked like a vampire who had been standing in a strong wind for a very long time, centuries perhaps.

"We should get back."

She nodded. The moment had passed. The only understanding that had been reached was that she desired him and he desired her, and that the realm world had no place for a human female in a mastyr vampire's life.

As he turned to offer his arm, however, a strange keening sound broke through the forest, a sound that seemed to come from everywhere and nowhere at once.

Abigail turned toward the sound and watched as a red mist moved between the trees toward the reception.

"Red wind," she whispered.

His gaze shot to her once more. "You can see that?"

She nodded.

He turned back as well. "The Invictus are here. Dear Goddess help us this night."

*** *** ***

"I will path you," Gerrod said. "It's the fastest way. Do you trust me?"

She blinked as though surprised. "Yes, of course."

He didn't exactly have time to explain. He slid his arm around her waist, dragged her against his side, lifted her off her feet, and sped back to the reception.

Her hand clutched his soft shirt, but other than a small, 'oh,' she didn't offer a single protest.

Five seconds later, he took her to Augustus. "The Invictus are coming. See to everyone."

"Yes, Mastyr."

He turned to Abigail. "Go with Gus."

She nodded in several quick bobs of her head.

He looked around, still holding her hand. There were at least three hundred realm-folk at the festivities, including the caterers and musicians.

He telepathed Jason. *How far away are you?*

Seven minutes.

Hurry. We've got Invictus sign.

He looked down at Abigail's hand not understanding why he was so damn reluctant to let it go. He met her gaze and saw in her eyes so much compassion that he had to look away.

Finally, he released her hand. "Go to the castle with Gus. Go quickly."

Again, she did nothing more than nod in agreement as though she understood. Well, she had been in and out of Merhaine for a year now and she had numerous realm friends. She would have heard many times about the Invictus. She would understand the trouble they faced.

"Go," she said softly. "Do what you do best."

He searched her gaze. Satisfied that she truly was all right, he turned on his heel and headed straight for the groom. He spoke swiftly to him. Gillet handed him the microphone.

He faced the people he knew so well. The red wind drew closer, flowing through the trees, brightening. He was always surprised that so few could see it.

"The Invictus are upon us. Please move into the castle with all due haste. Stay away from the forest. No one will be safe there. I will create a shield."

He heard Gus calling out in a powerful voice, bidding the guests follow him. The wedding party began to move, a little slow at first, as though stunned. But soon, those closest to the castle were running.

Once the crowd was past him, he began spreading his power off to each side, high in the air, wider and wider, a barrier of protection. The Invictus would not be able to pass, but would be forced to do battle with him. As he had done for the past century and a half, since he had reached mastyr vampire status, he gathered his battling power.

And there they were, at least twenty powerful Invictus wraith pairs. Their mates came to do battle as well, some vampires, a couple of trolls, several fae, and one elf. But all were soldiers now. Most of the realm-folk that had made the decision to bond with a wraith, sported spiked hair and gold loops hanging from their ears. All were air-borne in a strong form of levitation. Apparently, pairing with a wraith to form Invictus sharpened all powers. Blades of varying kinds were the weapon of choice.

As though the numerous pairs acted as one, the blades began to spin and then fly toward him. The massive shield held, deflecting the blades, which made it possible for him to bring his battling power down his arms, readying at the tips of his fingers, the frequency vibrating strongly. Once he was warmed up, the same power would also fly in scattered blasts from his chest, shoulders and arms.

The real battle commenced as he released his frequency power in bursts of focused killing energy. He moved his arms and hands swiftly, aiming for the wraiths who had the greater battling skill. The wraiths, however, had their own frequency energy and began to answer his powerful strikes, so that soon he saw dozens of red streams of light flying toward him again and again.

Though his shield held and kept him safe, each hit weakened him in the depths of his battle energy. He wouldn't be able to do this forever.

He hoped to hell that Jason arrived soon.

Chapter Two

Abigail trotted at the edge of the crowd, but saw something streak off to her left.

She glanced into the forest and saw a young troll child smile and dash behind a tree. The boy was playing.

She didn't take even a second to assess the situation, but did the only thing she knew to do. She ran straight for him and tried to take his hand, but he drew back. "You're human. I'm not supposed to speak to humans."

He ran farther away, deeper into the forest, in the direction of the Invictus. She called to him, but he didn't stop, not until she called out, "The Invictus are here, little one. Please come to me."

At that the boy stopped and turned toward her, his eyes wide. "Invictus?"

She nodded. "Mastyr Gerrod wants everyone in the castle. Now. Come to the castle."

He ran toward her, but again, she saw another streak of

movement. This time, however, it was the red wind. "Oh, no."

The boy ran into her arms and started to cry. He looked up and screamed. A wraith was close, maybe twenty feet away. She could feel Gerrod's power, she could even see it a few feet away. It was a huge wall of shimmering blue energy. But the wraith had been exploring the same phenomenon and had found the outer reaches, right where she stood.

Gerrod, she pathed. *I am west of you and I have a troll child with me. Can you shift your power another ten feet and cover us?*

She pulled the boy against a tree and held him tight. She looked up once more.

The wraith was a fierce-looking creature, almost opaque, with small eyes, yellow fangs and dark lips. This one, a female, was covered in red gauze-like strips of fabric, sewn loosely together, but floating easily around her long thin legs. She was barefoot and in flight, which was a wraith's preference most of the time.

She smiled, showing red gums.

Gerrod?

I'm trying Abigail, but I'm battling three Invictus. Can you reach a position where I can see you? Then I'll know better what to do.

The wraith taunted her, shifting back and forth through the air. "A human caught in the forest. What am I to do?" She laughed, almost a cackle.

Abigail lifted her chin and stood up. She knew this could be the end of her life, but she had to do something. Still holding the boy against her legs, she moved a foot forward then another. "What do you want with a human, wraith? I am nothing to you."

"Human blood tastes quite good." She hissed and bared her

fangs a little more.

Gerrod, can you see me yet?

No.

She took another step, then another, each putting her closer to the wraith. A couple more feet and she would reach a pool of light cast by the distant flood-lights which was also in line with Gerrod's shield.

"Why don't you battle those who have weapons?" Abigail called out, hoping to distract the wraith into a conversation. "Or are you just a coward, like all of your kind?"

The wraith's clothing stilled and she advanced forward, as Abigail advanced. Abigail put her foot in the beam of light, then brought the other one forward, the troll still hidden in the skirts of her gown, but he wept against her leg. He'd seen the wraith and he could hear her hiss.

"Foolish human. I won't just take your blood. I'll tear each of your limbs off just for the pleasure of it."

She launched, but at the same time, Gerrod's voice streaked through her head. *I've got you.* His power shield slipped between them and the wraith collided into that shield, as though she'd struck a brick wall.

Abigail heard a terrible crunching sound, the wraith's eyes rolled, then she plummeted to the ground falling hard. She didn't move.

Stay where you are. You will be safe.

She dropped to the ground and drew the boy onto her lap, holding him close. Gerrod's power wrapped around them. She could see him now. He moved like lightning in the distance, well above the ground as he made use of his levitation power.

Pulsing lights flashed from his arms, hands and shoulders in powerful streaks. Each time, a wraith screeched and fell, or one of the Invictus realm-folk cried out in pain then toppled over. The wraiths still fighting sent repeated red streaks of energy toward Gerrod. Each one hit his shield which protected him, but even she could see that his shield had holes in it here and there.

The flash of lights grew quicker.

Then suddenly, another Guard appeared, dropping from high in the sky, to levitate beside Gerrod. The lights flashed faster now and within another minute, the last of the Invictus lay on the ground.

Abigail rose, helping the boy to slide off her lap. She could hear a woman screaming in the distance, calling for 'Petrus'.

"That's my mama."

He pulled against Abigail's hand, but she didn't let him go. Instead, she began to run in the direction of the castle with him. But one last glance in Gerrod's direction revealed that all of the Invictus pairs lay dead in front of the ruined wedding cake.

*** *** ***

Gerrod was breathing hard and so damn weak. He had used up a tremendous amount of energy. He'd never seen so many wraith-pairs before and all well-armed. As his shield had weakened, he'd gotten nicked a couple of times, nothing serious but he was damn glad Jason had shown up when he did.

He glanced behind him and saw Abigail running with her hand clasped around a troll boy's hand. Until that moment the reality of her plight hadn't sunk in. Sweet Goddess she could have been killed.

He brought his power shield back toward him, reabsorbing as much of the energy as possible.

Jason sat down on the ground to catch his breath. Gerrod knew he had pushed hard to get here. They had both used up some serious reserves.

Jason looked up at him and pushed his light brown hair off his face. He wiped sweat from his forehead with the woven sleeve of his shirt. "That was fucking close, wasn't it?"

Gerrod nodded. "Very. There were forty in all."

"Sweet Goddess. What has happened? How have the Invictus grown in such numbers? Someone must have charge of them. I've never known these pairs to join together like this."

"I know. I have thought the very same thing." Gerrod swallowed hard. His left hand trembled, a sure sign that his blood-starvation was reaching a critical point. He should have summoned one of his *doneuses* to stabilize him long before tonight, but he hated to disturb the women. Each of his three donors were married to good men. The act seemed disloyal and he despised having to ask.

Though it wouldn't have mattered. He could have had a dozen *doneuses*, as some of his fellow mastyr vampires did, but he would still suffer from starvation. It was the curse of his 'mastyr' status. Though he, like all mastyr vampires, had tried a hundred remedies, the starvation remained. Although, with so few *doneuses*, he tended to reach dangerous levels much more often than those mastyrs with larger blood-harems.

The rest of the Guard began arriving, which helped his spirits since he had no doubt that once the notables in attendance at the wedding reached his entrance hall, cell-phones would light up alerting the media to the attack. It was only a matter of time before the TV station vans and reporters arrived.

The headlines the next day would be terrible, no doubt, but he thought it the wiser course to let the populace know that the Invictus had become active again. Parents would take extra precautions, neighborhood watches would be on guard again, and all volunteer policing units would gather with city entities to organize for increased patrols.

In the meantime, clean-up was critical. Each of the Invictus would have to be hauled to a morgue, families of any of those realm-folk who had paired with a wraith would have to be notified of the death. None of it was an easy task.

Gerrod issued his orders. And as Jason nodded then returned to the battlefield to begin the horrific disposal process, Gerrod headed to the castle to confer with those governing officials who had been present at the wedding. Each would of course have a great deal to say about how the governance of Merhaine ought to be conducted.

He repressed a sigh as the weight of rule descended heavily on his shoulders once more. Another tremor vibrated through his left hand and he made a fist then released it a number of times. He really didn't want a group of Merhaine dignitaries to observe him in this weakened state.

But as he walked up the broad front path to the castle, his thoughts turned to Abigail. His heart seemed to lumber in his chest. An image flashed through his mind of his fangs buried in her neck. Whatever the reason, more than life itself he wanted to know what her blood tasted like, if it would carry the flavor of rosemary, the scent that seemed to be attached to her always.

Yes, in the year he'd known her, he'd come very close to

obsessing about the damn human.

*** *** ***

An hour later, Abigail frowned as Gerrod marched away from her.

He had said very little to her except to insist she return to Flagstaff and not to come back because Merhaine was no place for a human.

She hadn't known exactly what to expect when she saw Gerrod next, but these terse commands weren't it. For one thing, she had wanted to thank him for saving her life but he hadn't given her the smallest opportunity.

For another, she really wanted to know what was happening.

She might even have demanded he speak with her for a moment, since he'd kissed her in the forest, but she saw that his shoulders were tight and his hands were balled into fists. He was struggling with a very difficult situation.

Most of the guests had driven back to their respective homes, but the castle entrance hall was still full of the more exalted citizens of Merhaine. He might have just battled forty Invictus, but now he had to put a different hat on, the one that would strive to reassure the worried mayors and council members of the various Merhaine cities that all would be well.

She'd been connected with Merhaine for a year now, increasingly so in the past several months because of the bakery she and her business partner, Elena, were due to open in the next few weeks.

Merhaine, one of the Nine Realms of North America. She was used to the existence of the realm world, as most humans were, at least those who were on the Internet with any consistency. The discovery of the realms some thirty years ago, before she was even born, had taken Earth by storm especially since the parallel nature meant that Realm and Earth cultures shared many things in common, from simple bonding rituals like marriage to much more complex things like language.

English was prevalent throughout the Nine Realms and the now inter-connected planes and the sharing of history and culture had even broadened realm-dialects.

Gerrod, on the other hand, was over three-hundred-years-old so that his speech patterns still hadn't caught up to the current Flagstaff vernacular. But she had seen other mastyr vampires interviewed from all over the United States' plane. Some of them, like Mastyr Ethan of the Bergisson Realm, spoke like most of the cops she knew, with a fair sprinkling of Earth-based profanity. How and why the revelation of a connected parallel plane had occurred at this point in Earth history was not something even the most brilliant scientists had yet to figure out.

But here Realm was and because of her bakery, she'd spoken to numerous trolls, fae, and elves about Mastyr Gerrod, about Merhaine, about all the various species that existed on this parallel plane.

Trolls were the most helpful, however, being extremely garrulous. In fact, the saying among realm was that if you kept a secret like a troll, it meant you never kept a secret, that you couldn't keep a secret if your life depended on it.

"Ask me."

Abigail turned to Augustus who was Gerrod's Master of the Household. She was alone with him now, in the hall not far from the shouting that had begun in the entrance hall.

Gus, as he was known, side-stepped like a child who had to go to the bathroom, but this she'd gotten used to as well. Trolls showed enthusiasm as well as many other emotions with their feet. Given that most trolls had lovely feet, contrary to human depictions, she thought all that movement fascinating.

Gus was five-six, which meant tall for a troll. He was also quite good-looking, with long light brown hair combed stylishly away from his face. She hadn't thought trolls could be handsome but in fact they were like any specie, running the gamut from homely to stunning. Gus ranged at the upper end, his blue eyes fringed in long lashes. The three ridges of his forehead had elegant turns.

Yes, much of Merhaine had become very familiar to her.

His eyes held such a light that despite all that had happened, Abigail smiled. "Yes," she said, answering the question he hadn't asked. "I want to know everything."

He smiled, his eyes now shining like stars. Did a troll love anything better than disseminating information? She didn't think so. Maybe not even better than her cupcakes and trolls were known for their sweet-tooths. This was one reason a troll made an excellent household governor but a very poor secretary.

He led the way to the far side of the castle, well away from the shouts now rolling from the entrance hall, to the northern wing that housed a massive kitchen, an equally long state dining room, and in the northwest, a lovely family breakfast room full of windows.

Because of the Invictus attack, the blinds were drawn. Otherwise, she knew that the forest had been illuminated with a thousand lights and was very pretty, another reminder that much of Merhaine life was lived at night.

He waved her to a chair by the hearth, in which burned a large log fire and after a few minutes, returned with tea service in white and green ivy.

Because she had come to the castle often to chat with him when she delivered her orders from her bakery, he knew how she liked her tea. He handed her the cup and saucer, prepared his own, then sat down.

The tea was redolent of cloves and cardamom. Now what was that novel she had read recently where the hero of the story, a great warrior, had smelled of cardamom. It was something like 'Ascending' or 'Accelerating', she couldn't quite remember. She had enjoyed reading that version of vampires. But how strange that now she was caught in her own world of not just vampires, but about every childhood tale she had ever heard of.

Gus's feet manipulated the footstool with the skill of his hundred and thirty years, until he was perfectly comfortable. All realm-folk were long-lived, which meant that Gus was still fairly young by Merhaine standards.

He met her gaze and lifted a brow.

This was her cue. She took a deep breath. "Why did the mastyr dismiss me?"

"Ah, the best question first. I like that. He told you to leave the castle because he is feeling too much for you, and you must trust me in this. I have known Mastyr Gerrod most of my life. You are the only castle supplier he ever seeks out. And the strangest thing is, he seems to know the moment you have come. Have you not noticed that he often brings an entire army to help you unload a few boxes of cupcakes?"

"I thought that was your doing?"

Gus chuckled. "And he always insists you stay for tea, have you not noticed that?"

"But he never sits down with me."

Gus appeared to be very knowledgeable as he nodded his head slowly. "But he hovers. Once you leave, I often find him standing about the great room." He gestured to a shorter hall behind her that led to the massive room where an annual fae ball was held.

She frowned. "He really does that?"

Gus nodded. "I don't think the mastyr quite understands his feelings at this point."

Gerrod felt too much for her? She wanted to know more, but the subject seemed too personal to her, as though Gus was sharing private things Gerrod wouldn't want her to know about. Gus might have few scruples about *sharing everything*, but she decided to draw the line.

Instead, she took a sip of tea, then asked, "Has he always been so tense?"

Gus sighed, his shoulders drooping. "Always. Since I have known him. He bears the burden of the entire realm on his shoulders." He brought his teacup to his lips and drank. Trolls tended to drink their tea in hearty gulps.

"But why is that? I mean I know that he has a lot of battling power so that he can fight the Invictus, but why isn't there a government in place to support him?"

Gus snorted. "Have you not been in Merhaine a year now? Do you not see the greater problem?"

She was afraid to give her opinion. She didn't know if it was politically correct to speak of the differences in the species. There was a lot of intermarriage among realm-folk, but it was still in the range of ten to fifteen percent, which meant that a majority could still be hostile and disapproving.

"Well," she began, trying for tact, "I have noticed that fights tend to break out between trolls and elves, elves and fae, fae and shifters, shifters and vampires. I even watched a forest gremlin start shouting at a fae who was ten times his size."

He nodded several times slowly. "Then you understand. Each folk believes they are the smartest, the best, the most reasonable, the strongest, the prettiest, you name it. And the older the realm individual, the more profound the belief in superiority."

"Oh, yes, I saw a fae woman spit on the ground in front of a troll. I was later told she was over five-hundred-years-old."

He shook his head, pinching his lips tightly together. He took another drink of tea, the three ridges of his forehead folding into a scowl. "We are not a perfect society. And though being long-lived has a wonderful advantage, it is even harder to rid our world of its deepest prejudices."

"Like a human dating a vampire?"

He met her gaze and his forehead relaxed, though a solemn light entered his eye. "Especially a vampire, not to mention a mastyr vampire."

"You would disapprove, then?" She leaned forward and took another sip.

"Thirty years ago, yes. Today, I don't know. I have come to know your kind and you are not as…well…as ignorant as I had supposed, or as cruel."

She wasn't offended. How could she be? "There is great cruelty in our culture."

"But much goodness as well."

She met his gaze once more. Because she wanted to understand the position of the castle staff, and especially Gus's take on the subject, she said, "Gerrod kissed me this evening."

Gus's eyes went wide.

She couldn't help but laugh. She knew his gossipy kind well, but she also knew something else. He was a wise troll and she trusted him, so she added, "I kissed him back."

His eyes literally moved in a complete circle, as though he was trying to wrap his mind around a certain thought. Or perhaps he was just wondering how the hell he could keep this a secret.

Since he didn't respond right away, she thought she would be more direct about what she wanted to know. "Do you disapprove? Is this a very bad thing?"

Finally, he set his cup and saucer back on the table, and bid her do the same. "Come with me. There is something I wish you to see."

She was on her feet and moving swiftly. Trolls were fast, those feet again.

The return walk in the direction of the entrance hall took at least a couple of minutes. The castle, as the dwelling was called, was more like an ancient European church, made of stone, with only one level, but having several extremely tall, and quite beautiful, vaulted ceilings.

Because of the gray stone, however, it definitely had the feel of a castle, especially with several suits of armor, imported from Medieval England, standing like sentinels near several of the doorways.

She thought he meant to take her straight into the entrance

hall, where a lot of shouting could be heard. Instead, he turned into a shallow alcove about twenty feet from the doorway. She frowned, wondering what he was doing. But he shoved the small table to the right and slid his hand up the left side wall.

She heard a click, then the wall moved inward a few inches. He pushed and gestured for her to precede him.

The room was pitch black but as had happened in the forest, her vision altered and changed and she could actually see as though the room had a glow. Was this some kind of fae magic, a spell that had been cast over the room? Or was this something she was actually doing?

Ever since she'd come to Merhaine, small things like this had begun happening to her. She wanted to ask Gus about it, but he seemed suddenly tense and waved her to the sofa that faced very strangely toward the wall adjacent to the entrance hall.

She sat down. He fiddled with the drapes that spanned most of the wall, pulling them back slowly. What a surprise when the entire entrance hall came into view as through a soft haze. She could see everyone and when Gus flipped a switch off to the right, she could hear everyone as well.

How was this done?

"Don't worry. We can't be heard but I can see your question. How is it done?"

She nodded.

He gestured with a sweep of his arm the length of the viewing window. "You know that big landscape in the entrance hall? It's painted on a very fine mesh screen."

"Oh, I see. Do you come here often to observe?"

"No, not often."

Gerrod had his back to the wall. He turned slowly until he was almost facing the painting. Then he was in her mind. *Abigail? Are you in the viewing room?*

She was so startled, she jerked in her seat. She also felt as though she was spying on him. *Yes, I'm here. How did you know?*

Not sure, just a feeling. His brow puckered, a familiar sight.

Gus brought me here, she explained. *Should I leave?* Please say no.

Stay if you like. You'll learn another reason why I want you to leave.

There was more than one reason?

He turned back into the room but stepped off to the side in a very casual manner so that she had a better view of what was going on. The room was full of notables. She recognized them from having read the various Merhaine newspapers.

But in the middle, beneath a very large round wood chandelier, a fae and an elf, both male, stood almost touching chests. Did she hear growls?

"Humans are vermin," the elf said.

"That's absurd. There are good humans and bad humans. The baker is quite acceptable. I think she smiles too much, but beyond that her intelligence is sufficient and her cupcakes are quite good, excellent in fact."

"Here, here," moved about the room.

But others grumbled.

Abigail wasn't hearing anything new, perhaps not as vehement as usual, but humans weren't universally accepted.

The elf continued. "You allowed this. You made a push to pass through all the permits for her bakery and I'll bet you a bushel of fall apples that she's the one that brought the Invictus tonight."

Abigail couldn't have been more surprised. How on earth did her presence at a fae wedding bring on an attack of the Invictus?

Gus elbowed her. "Don't listen to that. There's always some dimwit in the crowd that will cast another as a scapegoat for any bad occurrence. A few thousand years ago, he'd be the sort to throw his own child into a volcano in hopes of getting the gods to stop the neighboring tribe from marauding."

"What a lovely image."

Gus laughed. "But true, no?"

It was at this point, however, that the entire assembly of civic leaders started shouting, making their points with flying hands. Several trolls were dancing on their feet, leaping side to side, faces red.

Abigail glanced at Gerrod, ready to offer a telepathic joke, but she was stopped by the fierce look on his face and the way his hands had balled up.

"Enough," he shouted.

The room fell silent.

"We almost lost a child tonight, but thanks to Mistress Abigail's courage, the boy lives.

"We need to stay on point that this recent incursion won't be the last. We have more critical things to resolve than the presence of a bakery in our midst. Please return to your homes and we'll begin the process of developing strategies and organizing our civic volunteer Guard. I've brought out all the Guard to patrol through the night, but with forty dead, the Invictus won't hurry back, that much I can promise you."

Abigail knew that the Invictus were more of a deadly gang

than a marauding army. She also understood, however, that what happened tonight had never happened before.

The crowd muttered but began to ease toward the large castle door in the southeastern corner of the room, as though the plug to a drain had been pulled.

She glanced back at Gerrod and saw that his left hand twitched. He shook it slightly and even rubbed his hands together. When he released his hand, and the strange shaking continued, he shoved his hand into the deep pocket of his leathers.

"What's wrong with his hand?" Abigail asked.

"Did you see something?"

"A twitch. A tremor maybe."

Gus sighed, a deep rush of air. "This isn't good. I need to contact one of his *doneuses*."

Abigail felt light-headed suddenly. She knew what a *doneuse* was, a polite French expression that meant blood donor in Realm terms. She wanted to protest. She felt strangely protective of Gerrod suddenly. He'd kissed her. She didn't want another woman, no matter the specie, offering up her wrist or her neck or any other vein of her body, to the Mastyr of Merhaine.

That was her job.

That was her job?

What on earth was she thinking?

But certain pieces of this weird puzzle began to fall into place, how drawn she was to Gerrod, that she could communicate telepathically with him, that she could access his personal frequency. She could no longer deny that she had a serious connection to this man, to this vampire. She didn't know what it was, but the thought that he needed to take blood, reminded her of how sluggish her blood always felt, especially in Merhaine, as though her body had decided all on its own that she needed to be Gerrod's *doneuse*.

She sighed. But what did all of this mean? Could she donate her blood? Part of her shouted a resounding *yes*. But another part was much more sensible and seemed to stand, hands on hips, and say, *Vampires? Really?*

Gerrod was right. She needed to go home and she really did need to rethink the Hollow Tree bakery, especially with tonight's horrible turn of events in which, thanks to Gerrod and his Guard, no one at the wedding died.

Her thoughts turned to her sister. Abigail had been Megan's caregiver for the past nine years. Well, to be fair not exactly nine. After all, Megan had gotten married three years ago to a wonderful man and she'd birthed two children in the process.

But she believed she would always feel a profound sense of responsibility toward Megan. Her sister had been sickly most of her life and when their parents died those nine years ago, Abigail had been able to keep them together as a family because she'd been eighteen. Life insurance had paid off the house, and had given them funds to get through the early years, then later to open the bakery. Of course, Abigail had worked full-time as well, but she had always felt blessed that she and Megan had been able to stay together.

But Megan hadn't been well those first four years, in and out of the hospital with breathing difficulties, a chronic case of asthma that had taken her to the emergency room numerous times.

Much of that was behind Abigail now and in-between, she and her sister had built the bakery together. The expansion into Merhaine had been because of their extensive troll and elf customers. For the past three years the castle alone had been a major part of their success, which had led Abigail here, staring at Gerrod's back, at the constant tension in his shoulders, at the fact that he still held his hand deep in the pocket of his battle-leathers.

"He's always blood-starved, you know."

She put a hand to her chest, aware of her laden heart all over again. She had developed a strange medical condition in which her body produced too much blood. The doctors still didn't know what to make of it but she had become a regular and welcome donor to the Flagstaff blood bank.

Abigail turned toward Gus. He rose to his feet and looked down at her. She could barely make out his features. "Why is that? Why is he always blood-starved if he has donors?"

Gus shrugged. "Something about being a mastyr vampire. They're all blood-starved in the Nine Realms, the mastyr vampires who rule. Although, I don't know about any of the other Continents. He even has three *doneuses*, but he hates to use them. They're all married. He feels like it's a violation."

"Okay, so how long has he been blood-starved? I know he's three-hundred-years-old. Tell me it hasn't been that long?"

Gus shrugged. "Not sure. I think he reached mastyr status a hundred and fifty years ago, but there had to have been a long transition. I can't believe he'd just suddenly be starved."

"So, why doesn't he just get more *doneuses*, add to his little harem, and take more blood?"

Gus just stared at her. "Well, you'd probably have to ask him that, but I wouldn't. There's more to blood-taking than I think you or I can understand. I think it's one reason the vampires hate the Invictus wraiths as much as they do." He turned to close the curtains across the wide landscape at the now empty room and flipped off the switch. "Because the victims are unwilling, I've heard them call it a blood-rape."

"Oh, God."

"Yes, exactly."

The door opened and light from the hall formed a rectangle of yellow on the floor behind the couch shaded by Gerrod's massive shadow. Funny, she always seemed to forget how big he was until he stood in a doorway. He filled it from side to side, the top jamb clearing his head by only a few inches.

He held his left hand in his right now, and rubbed his wrist back and forth. "Everything okay?"

His voice was a deep hole.

"Sure," she said. But what Gus had told her had knocked her out of stride.

She was about to ask to be taken back to Flagstaff, but Gus was before her. "I'm putting Mistress Abigail in one of the guest rooms."

Gerrod looked around. "She should go back to Flagstaff."

"It's a long trip by car and all the way east. Is there a Guard in that direction? Someone watching the plane access point?"

Gerrod shook his head. "We have never needed guards at the access before." He scowled, harder now. "Very well. We certainly have enough guest rooms."

He backed into the hall and Abigail followed him.

He stood aside watching her carefully, very guarded. She wanted to say something to him, to offer some comfort, but no words came. Since he made no move to invite her to chat, even a little, she turned in the direction of the north rooms away from Gerrod. Gus hurried to move in front of her, leading the way.

"I'll bid you good-night," Gerrod called out.

Abigail stopped and turned toward him. By now, he stood beside his library door. She lifted a hand, still feeling so strange after having heard about his blood-starvation and why hadn't she known of it? Although, honestly it explained a helluva lot about his perpetual irritability. Men needed to be fed. She was sure that axiom was as true in the realm world as it was in Flagstaff. Megan's husband got a lot louder when his blood-sugar bottomed out.

As she turned back to follow Gus, her thoughts started tumbling around until at last she caught up with him and asked, "What does Gerrod usually do now, after a battle like this? Does he go to bed?"

"No, he'll probably call for a bottle of whiskey, drink about a third of it, and pass out in one of the big chairs in front of the fire in the entrance hall. It's sort of a ritual."

"I guess he would deserve at least that much," she said, but her footsteps grew slower and slower, until she stopped altogether.

Gus turned back to her, his three ridges floating upward, questioning.

Her right shoulder now faced back down the hall. She could see the light from the library flicker as though Gerrod walked back and forth in front of a lamp, pacing.

"Is everything all right?" Gus asked.

"Just give me a sec." She headed back in the direction of the library. Her heart was slamming in her chest because she had never done anything like this in her life.

When she reached the doorway, she had meant to walk right

up to him and ask him a few pointed questions, but she couldn't. Gerrod now sat in his chair, his elbows on the massive central table, his head in his hands. He rocked slowly, back and forth as if in great pain.

Oh. God.

Something inside her settled very deep, maybe falling into that hole that was his voice, or maybe she was just feeling all his pain on some kind of vampire frequency he was emitting right now, she wasn't sure.

But a decision came to her, though she felt strongly it had to be just for this night, this one night.

She retraced her steps up the hall, rejoining Gus.

For the past year, she had seen Gerrod in more than a dozen settings, consoling a mother who had lost a son, kissing a grandmother on her cheek, offering stern but solid advice to a younger Guardsman, teasing Augustus. She wondered if this was the true basis for her attraction to him, that on some level she knew the vampire and knew him well. His character showed in everything he did and all that he was, every word he spoke, every soft touch on a shoulder, every sympathetic gesture.

Abigail blinked. She couldn't believe she was going to do this, but after seeing Gerrod in a shattered state in the library, she had to. Besides, her blood had that thick feeling again, almost lumpish as she liked to think of it. Though she never really felt in danger of a heart attack or anything, she did feel a pressing need to give some of it away. And right now she might just have a solution that didn't involve donating to the blood bank.

"Come with me, Gus. I want you to show me to the mastyr's bedroom."

Gus's brows rose almost to his upper ridge. But after staring at her for a long moment, he nodded very firmly, then said, "Yes, mistress. If you will follow me."

Once in his bedroom, which she knew well from the tour he'd given her many months ago, she said, "And where is the bathroom?"

Gus led her into a side chamber, very deep with a huge copper tub. She drew near, leaned over and pushed the plug in hard. She turned the water on adjusting until the temperature was on the hot side.

"Where are the herbs he bathes in?"

"Herbs, Mistress?"

"Yes, he always—" She felt her cheeks grow warm. That she always smelled Gerrod, and that his scent reminded her of fresh rain in the forest, was not something she intended to reveal to Gus. "That is, where is the soap he would ordinarily use?"

"Ah." He moved over to the shower and brought a bottle of gel, an amber color.

Abigail took it and sniffed the spout. But it didn't smell like fresh rain. "Towels?" she asked.

As she watched the steam rise from the copper tub, she laughed. "Gus, there is something more. Do vampires like hot water, I mean hot like this?"

Gus smiled and his smile broadened to a grin. "Very much. Ah, mistress, you have gladdened my heart."

"And now, there is one more thing I should like, then I'm hoping you will send all the staff to bed."

He blinked at least four times. Finally, he bowed to her. He actually bowed. Then he said, "Understood. And what is it you'd like me to do?"

"I should like a platter of fruit and cheese and your mastyr's favorite German sweet wine. Nothing more, or less, mind."

"Very good. Very good," he said.

"You will leave the platter outside the bedroom, in the mastyr's sitting room."

"Yes, yes, of course."

"And I am asking for complete discretion."

At that, he blinked as though not understanding. "Discretion?"

Abigail bit back her smile. She couldn't think why she had bothered asking for his discretion. She might as well have asked him to cut off his right arm. "Well, try for a reduced narrative."

He screwed up his lips.

"Oh, very well. Speak as you will."

"Yes, mistress." But he grinned.

She sighed. She had set her feet on this course, and there was nothing to be done now. No doubt by tomorrow afternoon, when the staff rose early for the night, the entire castle would know she had spent the early morning hours in the Mastyr's rooms, that is, if Gerrod permitted her to stay.

Abigail waited until the tub was sufficiently full which wasn't very long. Given Gerrod's size, he would displace a lot of the water. When she had turned the faucets off, she steeled herself for what she had to do next and for what she wanted to do more than anything else in the world, Realm or otherwise.

When she reached the doorway of the bedroom, before moving into Gerrod's private sitting room, she removed her heels and placed them by the door, well out of the way. She really didn't want Gerrod tripping over her shoes.

Chapter Three

Gerrod sat at the map table, elbows on the hard wood, his head in his hands. Fatigue wasn't the only thing he felt, but a terrible despair. He couldn't seem to put the images of the attack out of his mind nor could he imagine when this madness would end.

Never, was the only thing that came to mind.

And how was he to bear 'never'?

He heard a soft padding of feet in the hallway, very soft and unfamiliar. He lifted his head and felt the frequency of his battle power begin to charge, a low vibration deep in his gut.

His heart thrummed in his throat.

Had the Invictus somehow bypassed all his security measures and invaded the castle?

But red hair appeared, instead of red wind, and the soft clinging cream gown that Abigail still wore from the wedding.

Abigail, oh, dear Goddess, no.

"Why aren't you in your room?" The sudden burst of adrenaline, of fearing that an enemy had come to the castle, left him irritable once more. "You should be in bed, asleep."

But she strolled forward, now in her bare feet, as though she belonged in his house. "Just thought I'd have a look around."

He turned away from her, fatigue settling in hard. He wanted his whisky and the deep leather chair in front of the fire. Whisky always eased the tremor in his hand. He'd have to summon a *doneuse*, but not tonight. "Did you leave your room and forget your way? That part of the castle is a rabbit warren." He was trying to be polite but he wanted her gone so he wouldn't have to think about what he wanted to do to her, what he had almost done to her earlier.

"No, I didn't forget my way."

"Good, that's good. But you must be exhausted."

"Not so fatigued as you, I'm sure." He looked up at her at that. She was standing just a few feet away. The light from the lamp on his desk seemed to enhance her delicate complexion. She was very beautiful, almost ethereal because of her fair skin.

She held out her hand to him. "Come. I've made something for you. I think it's what you need. I'm not sure, but I believe it will do. Will you trust me?"

"This is a strange sequence of words coming from you." He narrowed his gaze. "Always the enigma. But I am too tired to decipher your meaning."

She smiled. An image drifted through his mind, something that felt as though it came from the future, probably just a fantasy. But she was in his bed, asleep on the pillow next to him.

He gave his head a shake. It was late, he had battled tonight, and now he was imagining things.

She had been a good sport and hadn't complained once during the attack. She had even saved the boy. He owed her this little bit, he supposed, despite how tired he was, to accept whatever kindness she had prepared for him.

He rose to his feet but didn't take her hand. He feared touching her. Since she was able to connect with his personal frequency, he didn't want to relive anything as dangerous as what he had shared with her earlier in the forest.

He swept his hand in the direction of the doorway. "Lead the way, Mistress Abigail."

She turned and without any hint of flirtation, began walking down the long hall. She was going in the opposite direction of the entrance hall, which meant he would have a long trek back to get to his whisky and sink into his leather chair.

But he had told her he would oblige her and so he would.

He only suspected something was wrong when she led him not in the direction of any of the public rooms, or even toward the guest suites of which there were twenty on the far side of the castle, but rather straight down the hall to his private quarters.

He stopped at the top of the hall. "Mistress Abigail, I believe you must have lost your way."

She didn't even pause in her steps as she looked over her shoulder and said, "No, I didn't. Come."

On she moved. He waited for a long moment even after she disappeared into his private sitting room. Which led to his bedroom.

He felt dizzy suddenly but not precisely fatigued. In fact, his heart had begun a serious pounding and all that activity within his chest put his booted feet in motion again. He was certain he shouldn't be walking down this hall, but he couldn't seem to help himself.

He didn't take many women to bed and never at the castle. Far too complicated. The Mastyr of Merhaine couldn't allow for expectations to arise in any quarter.

But this, a human. Could he engage with Abigail and not get caught in a different kind of net?

He passed through the sitting room. When he reached the angled doorway of his bedroom, he pushed the door wide against the stone wall. He glanced down and saw her matching cream heels sitting side-by-side, close together, very tidy.

He scanned the bedroom but she wasn't there.

He stood on the threshold, staring at his bed, his dresser, his massive closet. He had lived alone here for a hundred and fifty years. In all that time, he had never brought a woman into his private rooms.

He wanted to call out to Abigail, to tell her to leave at once. He even lifted his chin, parted his lips, but the words wouldn't come. Maybe he was just too damn tired.

His heart beat harder now and in the distance he heard water splashing.

Was the woman bathing? His body responded, just thinking thoughts of Abigail in his copper tub. Her long red hair, her beautiful eyes, her pale skin, would look almost exotic in his tub.

"Gerrod. It's all right. Come to me. Just this once. No pressure. No hidden motives. Nothing." Then her soft chuckle as though she found what she said amusing.

For some reason, perhaps the soft but confident tone of her

voice, his boots once more began to move. Some terrible threshold had been crossed in which his profound need, his fatigue, his despair overrode his fear of being involved with Abigail, with this human.

He moved into the bedroom. Looking through the archway into the bathroom, he saw that she sat on a stool at the lower end of the tub, near the faucet, and she had removed her gown. She wore an undergarment that also looked like a gown, but with thin straps. It covered her breasts and ended at her knees in a line of lace.

His desire for her rose, despite the fact that she was still essentially modestly clothed.

Essentially.

As he drew closer, he saw that her gown, which she had worn to the wedding, hung on one of the pegs to the left, opposite the tub.

He still hesitated. She had prepared him a bath. A great kindness, indeed.

He chose in that moment, not to over think any of it, not to have any expectations, not to try to take charge, not to do anything except to give himself over to this strange human.

He stood by the side of the tub and she rose from her stool. As she reached for the thick shoulder strap, she hesitated. She looked up at him. He nodded.

The moment she made contact with the silver buckle, he felt it again, his realm vibration, coming alive with her touch.

She snapped the large silver buckle that held the strap together. She caught one side and slid the rest off his back. She opened the coat wide, then spread her fingers over his left pec. Her lips parted.

"I can feel your vibration," she said. "It's powerful and seductive. It strikes me here in a steady rhythm." She looked back up at him and removed her hand from his chest and put it between her breasts.

He nodded. "We are a world of frequencies. Even when I battle, it's a frequency that I tap and I'm able to draw energy from the earth and from the air and form it into narrow beams that can do great harm.

"My personal frequency is a very different thing. When you touch it, as you just did, it's as though all that I am, to the end of each extremity, begins pulsing toward the center of my being." He laid a hand flat on his upper abdomen. "Here. Put your hand here."

She laid her hand against his stomach and her brows rose. "I can feel it all up my arm." Her lips were still parted as once more she met his gaze. "It's very sexual."

"It should be. It's called the mating frequency."

"Well, I won't deny that it fills me with desire, the way I felt in the forest earlier. So, have all the women you've known enjoyed your frequency?"

She was smiling, thinking she understood, but she didn't.

He shook his head slowly. "Never. I have to allow it to happen and I've never wanted to because it would mean a deeper connection. The women I have known couldn't do what you seem to do so easily, to access my personal vibration, which makes you a mystery I cannot solve."

She seemed truly shocked. "Then how the hell can I do this?"

"I do not know, Abigail. It worries me."

She nodded several times but fell silent. Finally, she said, "Very well, we can't understand everything right now but we'll just have to make the best of it." Then her smile appeared. His breath caught. He realized he loved her smile, that just seeing that bright display of even teeth, her expression full of nothing but good-will, eased his heart.

His own need for her grew. He was hard beneath his leathers, stiff with desire. Who was she that she could bring forth his frequency?

He removed the long leather, sleeveless coat. She took it from him and hung it on a peg next to her gown, as well as the shoulder strap.

She waved him to the stool. He sat down. She drew the rug close and knelt before him. She unbuckled his boots, another kindness. She leaned back and he slid them off, along with the thick socks. She took them from him and set them beneath his coat.

He unbuttoned the dozen small buttons that held the soft woven shirt together. He pulled the shirttails from the pants and let the garment slide from his shoulders.

Though he extended the shirt toward her, she stood staring at him. Of course she would never have seen him like this before and his pecs tightened and swelled, his shoulders and biceps flexed. He drew his stomach in tight. He was what the humans called 'built', muscled as all Guardsmen were.

Her pupils had dilated and through her slip he could see the taut beads of her nipples. She shared his desire.

She blinked a couple of times as though clearing her thoughts, then said, "You may remove your fighting leathers." She knew that was what they were called. He almost smiled.

He met her gaze as he took them off. He was naked as he

handed them to her. She folded them up but in so doing, some of the dried blood, and some not so dry from the nicks he had received, ended up on her arms and hands. Fortunately, he healed quickly and the various cuts were long gone.

She gasped, just a little, then squared her shoulders. She folded the pants and settled them beside the boots.

When he stood there, now fully aroused in front of a woman he desired, her gaze dipped to his erection then back to his eyes. She gestured to the tub and smiled. "Get in, Gerrod. And when you can tolerate it, sink beneath the water. I mean to wash your hair."

He was sore from battling and very tired. He was also weak from blood starvation. He stumbled getting in, but righted himself only to find her hand on his back as if to steady him. The gesture moved something in his heart and suddenly he hurt so deep that he wished her gone, wished he had never met her, wished she had kept her kindnesses to herself.

How long had it been since he had known such attention and care? Yes, his people were good to him and showed him many respectful tender gestures. But he never let anyone get this close that after a battle, he might be soothed.

He sank into the water, pulling the woven clasp from his hair and let it drop to the stone floor. "The temperature is perfect," he said. He didn't look at her until she leaned over and slid her hands in the water as well and began rinsing the blood from her arms. Then she drew close, hovering above his lips. He leaned up slightly, which encouraged her so that she came down to him the rest of the way and kissed him, a soft warm pressure, and so very welcome.

He sighed when she drew back. "Why are you doing this?"

"Because I have seen how you care for your people and I appreciate what you do. I have known you long enough, Gerrod, to understand that there is no one to comfort you. So I thought, just this once, I would do what I could, with no plan in mind other than to give you what I can this dawn, maybe to comfort you, if I could. But please don't worry. I have no purpose other than that, no hopes or intention for sharing a future with you. Rest assured, there is no obligation here except to enjoy the moment."

He nodded, closed his eyes and sank beneath the water, a sort of baptism. When he came up, she had moved behind him, having taken the stool with her. She washed his hair and it was one of the finest sensations he had ever known, her fingers scrubbing his scalp and working the soap through the difficult length. He rinsed by dipping again, but before she could apply a most necessary crème rinse, he rose up out of the bath and gestured to the shower. "This is my preference, but the bath was perfection."

She smiled. He began making his way to his shower and turned on all three shower heads. He stepped inside and shifted, only to find, much to his shock, that she had dispensed with her slip and her bra and was now stepping out of what looked like a beautiful black lace thong.

His body responded once more. Couldn't be helped on so many levels. He'd been in battle. A woman was what he wanted.

She didn't join him right away, however. Instead, she went to the sink and was busy there for about a minute. Curious, he watched her, as the vertical jets powered against the sore muscles of his back. She had a now damp thong in hand and hung it between two of the pegs on the wall where her gown and his coat hung.

His chest tightened. There was only one reason she would

have done so, that she meant to spend the day in his bed. It was such a practical, womanly thing to do, the way a woman who ran a successful business would always be thinking one step ahead, what needed to be done next.

If he'd had any doubts about the scope of her intentions, they disappeared as she moved toward the shower, her chin high and her nipples peaked.

What rose to the surface of his mind was simple. He had wanted her from the first moment he'd laid eyes on her and caught her delicate rosemary scent. He'd wanted her with a fervor that was even now beyond his comprehension.

He didn't try to hide how aroused he was. But he was a big man so he supported all that purposeful weight as she stepped in beside him.

He gave her room so that she could dip beneath the spray. All her pretty curls had already given way to the difficulties of the night and now her makeup, too, drifted in the direction of the drain.

He moved away from her and took his time memorizing each curve, the shape of her breasts, the exact pinkish hue of her areola, that her belly button seemed to collect the water before allowing it to flow down her abdomen and into the crease of her tender flesh. Her skin was milky, her legs shapely and long. Even her feet were pretty and he had a sudden desire to kiss them.

If he was to have only one night with her, then he would make the most of it.

She emerged from the spray and turned. She shampooed her hair and rinsed. He watched the bubbles float over her shoulders and down her arms. He became fascinated with how her breasts moved and what they looked like when she lifted her arms to squeeze the water from her hair, to shake her locks with her fingers trying to get the soap out.

When she was satisfied, she reached for the crème rinse. She applied it to her hair and once it had reached the tips, she turned to him and smiled. "You'll have to bend down a little. I'm not a short woman, but you're damn tall."

He smiled. My God, when was the last time he had smiled. His heart felt lighter. When had his heart ever felt lighter after a battle?

He had a sudden profound desire to find some place in the castle to keep her, to chain her up perhaps, so that whenever he needed to feel the weight of his responsibilities lift from his shoulders, he could go to her and she would make him smile.

He leaned over and she poured the crème rinse on his hair and worked it through every strand all the way to the ends as she had done her own hair.

He wanted to touch her, but she was all business. She rinsed her hair, then without a word, she left the shower. She dried off and wrapped her hair up, then simply padded from the bathroom, her bottom moving in the most exotic way as she disappeared from view.

Realizing he could no longer see her, that she had somehow escaped his touch, he felt panicky, afraid on some level that she would vanish. He almost stumbled from the shower and toweled off. He was still a bit damp in parts when he went into the bedroom.

He paused on the threshold. She was on the bed, the covers turned all the way back to the footboard, and still very naked. She was kneeling but sitting back on her heels. In front of her was a tray of fruit and cheese and two small glasses of white wine.

She had provided him an elegant feast. Did she understand what she was doing? What it meant to a man to have a woman feed him? Of course, she did own a bakery, so perhaps on a very intuitive level, she understood how critical it was to provide food to the community, even a realm community.

"Please, Gerrod, come and make yourself comfortable. If you don't want to eat, you don't have to, although there are other things besides these fruits and cheeses that might be equally palatable to you."

He had lived a long time.

He had heard double entendres in every form imaginable.

Maybe it was because she was naked, or that she had brought him food to eat, but these words pleased him to no end, and once more brought him to attention.

Her gaze fell. He had to support himself as he walked. He thumbed the tip of his cock and watched her eyes widen.

"I would feed you as well, Abigail, if it would please you."

Her nipples had become hard pebbles once more and a flush covered her cheeks. "I am very torn," she said. "For these figs look wonderful. But on the other hand, I want nothing more than to be fed." She unwound the towel from her damp curls and let it fall behind her.

"And so you shall be." He crawled across the bed, careful not to disturb the tray. He drew up beside her on his knees.

She turned her shoulder into him and planted her hand on his thigh. She leaned just a little and parted her lips.

He tilted his pelvis and slipped his cock into her mouth. He fed her slowly, one inch at a time. She didn't suck but held her tongue beneath him and moved in a little erotic ripple. He groaned. He pulled out then pushed in again slowly. He met her gaze as she looked up at him.

I feel your vibration, she said, tapping his telepathic frequency. *How does it feel?*

Wonderful. It's made my lips and tongue tingle.

Her mouth began to close around him and this time when he withdrew she suckled him. His back arched and he almost came.

He withdrew and took a series of strong breaths.

She didn't move. He believed she understood his dilemma.

"Imagine," she said at last.

He looked down at her. "Imagine what?"

"Imagine, I just had so much to eat, and yet I'm still hungry."

He chuckled.

"Now, why don't you stretch out on your side and let me feed you bits of fruit and cheese."

He ended up curling his large body around hers. She took her time and placed a slice of strawberry on his tongue. Then a little jack cheese. Apple and cheddar. Figs and gorgonzola. She handed him his glass of wine.

He drank.

She ate as well and drank.

He touched her waist and slid his hand down to caress her bottom. She arched as though it gave her pleasure so he kept his hand low.

When moisture collected at the tips and threatened to drip down her back, he wiped at her hair.

She did the same for him.

He was surprised how hungry he was, even more so when the

plate of food was finally gone.

He stared at the barren grape cluster. He had long-forgotten his wish to sit in his chair and drink whisky. This was better. He was feeling stronger.

He slipped off the bed, and took the tray to the stand near the door. He headed back but almost stumbled.

She was on her knees now, still on the bed, still very naked, and one hand rubbing between her thighs. Her gaze raked his body. So he moved slower, letting her look. He understood what the sight of his Guard body could do to a woman, the heavy muscles, his cock partially erect and growing.

Her gaze slipped over his pecs. Her lips parted. They were nearly ruby red as she licked them. Her gaze fell, dropping down his abs. She leaned forward slightly still fondling herself.

It appeared she was still hungry.

He rounded the bed and she knee-walked over to the side. Fortunately, the bed wasn't too tall, which meant she didn't have far to go. She planted her hands on his hips and lowered her head.

He was pretty sure that for any man, this was one of the most beautiful sights in the world, in any world, vampire, fae, troll, elven or human. Yes, any world.

She sucked him, licked him, swirled her tongue. He was upright now, hard as a rock. The food had been a good idea. He'd needed nourishment especially since his blood-starvation was reaching a critical point. He would need blood within twenty-four hours or he would become too weak to do anything, even to take blood. This could mean a quick slide toward death for any vampire.

For now, though, he was safe, but barely.

Her hands drifted down the sides of his legs, back up, around his buttocks. She squeezed. He groaned.

He couldn't believe this was happening, a woman in his room after all these decades. But this was what he'd needed, food and sex, and she'd delivered for no other reason than that she'd perceived his need and appreciated what he did for his people.

She leaned back on her heels and looked up at him. "There's something I want to tell you."

"What's that?" He stroked her cheek, thumbed the lips that had been suckling him.

"I've been seeing a doctor for the past year, since about the time I started coming to Merhaine."

He frowned. "Are you ill?"

"Not exactly. I have a blood condition none of the Arizona specialists can figure out. But I've wondered if my coming to Merhaine has had something to do with it."

His mouth quirked. "So, because you've been around vampires and other folk who need and enjoy the sharing of blood, you think your blood condition has something to do with that?"

"Maybe. But for the past year I've had what feels to me like lumpish blood."

He chuckled. "What do you mean 'lumpish'?"

"I suppose it's a strange word choice. Maybe more like sluggish. And my heart would pound as well. Both sensations, however, made me wonder what was going on, so I got checked out and that's when the doctor started taking my blood."

"You mean to have it tested?"

She shook her head. "To drain me of excess. It would seem I create excess blood for a human."

He jerked forward. He couldn't have heard right. "You produce too much blood and your medical doctor drains you of it?"

She nodded. "Yes, at certain times, especially after I've been to Merhaine. And it really feels that way right now." She took his hand and pressed it against the center of her chest between her breasts.

Her heart was pounding. He frowned. "I don't understand. Exactly how much blood would he take at any given time?" He thought maybe an ounce or two.

She drew a deep breath and said, "A pint."

He really couldn't have heard right. His balls tingled and his cock got even a little harder. She swept her hair away from the side of her neck. He weaved on his feet.

"I'm thinking maybe you could relieve me of some of that blood now."

A pint of blood, her lumpish blood, her pounding heart, his fucking blood-starvation.

Oh, damn all wraiths to hell, he needed this. "Are you sure?" His voice was hoarse like it had been shredded.

"Gerrod, is it normal for a specie different from vampires to create extra blood?"

He shook his head very slowly. "I've never heard of it before."

She scooted back on the bed, then stretched out, her damp hair still shoved away from her neck. She turned her head slightly. "I can feel the vein thumping away. Gerrod, will you try an experiment with me? Will you take some of my blood? I know you need some right now."

"Gus told you."

"I saw the tremor in your hand."

"Shit."

She met his gaze. "It is what it is, and I have weird blood.

Would you at least try? Maybe right now I'm what you need and I really think you're what I need." It didn't help that she slowly parted her legs.

He chuffed a hoarse sound, something like a growl, then crawled over her body, lying between her legs. "You've had experience?"

She smiled. "I had a boyfriend a few years ago. We enjoyed each other. A lot."

He wasn't as satisfied with this response as perhaps he should have been. He didn't like the idea of her with another man, any man, ever, not in the past, not in the future. He was being ridiculous since essentially, based on what she had said to him, this was what the humans called a one-night stand.

She slid her fingers around his cock and squeezed just so. The breath he drew shuddered. "Your vibration again," she said. "Like quick waves of energy. It's just amazing. My fingers are tingling."

"Yes," he whispered. He stared at her neck. The hunger that lived in him had become an old friend, someone he talked to, tried to cajole and often pleaded with. For the woman to lie there and be a promise that his hunger would be sated because she carried extra blood, seemed the height of impossibility.

But there was something more, the vibration he felt in his body was stronger now, a kind of humming that was fast growing into an ache up the insides of his thighs, a claiming kind of ache, something he had never quite experienced before, like he needed to enter this woman and hold her pinned to his bed.

But as he looked down at her, as he let his cock push against her lower flesh, this didn't feel all that simple to him. Abigail could make light of this, she could bare her neck, she could talk about having enjoyed sex, but he understood exactly what she'd done tonight. She'd taken him in hand and offered herself, even her blood, for no other reason than that she had seen that he struggled with life tonight and she wanted to ease him.

No, this was not simple.

"You've shown me an amazing amount of compassion, Abigail. I will never forget this."

He leaned down and put his lips on hers. The tingling of energy was stronger now. She released his cock and slid her arms around his back, moaning softly, her fingers exploring the muscles of his shoulders and arms. He lowered himself onto her and deepened the kiss.

She moaned again, a huskier sound this time, but drew back slightly. "All that constant vibration against my mouth, where your hands touch me, where your legs are connected, even your cock. Oh, Gerrod, we should have done this when I first came to the castle and never stopped."

He smiled as he kissed her again. She was right, the energy waves were very strong between them. He'd never known his mating frequency to feel so weighted. Usually it was just a faint hum, but this had power.

Her mouth was a sensual moist well and he savored, thrusting his tongue slowly, a foreshadowing of things to come, of things to 'enjoy'.

She suckled the end of his tongue and a shot of pleasure rose up within his abdomen, tugging hard. He thrust harder. She suckled harder.

He drew back and chuckled. It was all so enjoyable. He'd forgotten how wonderful this could be.

She smiled in return. "My God, you are so beautiful when you smile. It sort of curves up on one side more than the other. A half smile." She reached up and kissed the side that curved, then with her fingers played with his lips.

"Open," she whispered.

He parted his lips and her finger slid inside. He could feel his frequency vibration flow over her skin as she stroked his tongue. He suckled her finger, his gaze fixed on hers, those beautiful light-green eyes.

Oh, that tingling again, her voice whispered inside his head.

He released her finger. "I'm hungry," he said.

She started to say something, but he slid in a single quick glide down her body and took her mons in his mouth and swiped his tongue the length of all her tender femaleness.

Her body arched beneath his. "I didn't think it could get better, but your frequency is working me everywhere." She groaned this time. "I'm so close and we've barely started."

He pushed and licked and sucked. She began to thrash on the bed. He focused the waves of his power on all her tender flesh. A moment later, she was screaming at the ceiling and bucking against him. "Oh, God, oh, God, oh, God."

He kissed her and licked her. "More?" he asked when her hips settled back into the mattress.

"Yes."

He repeated the process, until her screams once more rang up to the rafters.

*** *** ***

Abigail lay against the sheets, one with the bed, the room, the rafters, and above all Gerrod. He was kissing her abdomen, each vibrating touch a promise of more to come.

She stroked his long damp hair, savoring the aftermath of the orgasms. How many? She might have lost count. She felt both satisfied yet ready for so much more since what he had just done to her was more appetizer than main course. She longed to feel him inside her, all that heavy rope of him.

She hadn't been with a man in a long time.

He now licked her navel and desire seemed to streak higher and lower at the same time, especially with that sensual wave of energy as skin met skin.

He climbed up the bed, kissing and suckling his way. He took as much of her breast in his mouth as he could and sucked.

She moaned. Then he held it in his mouth and just rubbed over the tip with his vibrating tongue. The pleasure of his touch seemed to pass through her in the same way as though caught on all those waves.

She reached low and found him, all that was male and Gerrod and so desirable.

She rubbed the soft sensitive crown and he groaned heavily. He released her breast and climbed a little higher over her. He pushed her hair back over her shoulder.

As though she understood, she exposed her neck to him and became aware, as she surrounded his cock with her hand, that her neck was throbbing. She felt a wetness on her neck first and realized it was his saliva. Then she felt his tongue.

The same vibration was there.

Abigail, your skin tastes so good, like rosemary.

Rosemary?

Yes.

She gently stroked him up and down. *Gerrod. You're so beautiful.*

I love your voice in my head. He groaned louder and began licking her neck and angling over her, preparing to strike.

Even your voice has a kind of pulsing energy, she said as his lips played over her skin. He sucked above her vein and a streak of pleasure like nothing she'd known before traveled straight down her body, into her well, and she spasmed hard.

She felt desperate to experience it all.

He must have known the pleasure he was giving since he was a vampire of age and experience. But the added waves of energy that came with his lips on her neck, his heavy muscular pecs against her breasts, his thighs against hers, was incredible.

I want to be inside you.

She held him now, her arms surrounding his shoulders. *Yes, please, I want you inside me.*

She shifted her hips. She was in agony. She felt the tip of his cock push. She wiggled and helped, moving around until he was able to enter her thrusting forward, pulling back. She was so wet that soon it was a dream of movement and the internal vibrations were so…*aaaaahhhh.*

He moved faster, a light quick speed that no human male could have accomplished.

The vibrations reached a crescendo and she came screaming all over again.

You're so tight. Oh, dear Goddess. He grunted, holding back, yet continuing to thrust until her orgasm receded. She was breathing hard and felt so wonderful except for one thing: Her heart pounded too hard in her chest.

"Gerrod, you have to take my blood. Now. My heart is beating too hard."

He should have warned her, but no doubt the intensity of her request prompted him. He struck her vein but because she hadn't known what to expect, she jerked and it hurt worse. Then he withdrew his fangs and began to suck. She could feel her blood flowing into his mouth and a whole new experience took over, a kind of euphoria.

She closed her eyes, and as his hips moved slowly, his cock in and out of her, and as her blood continued to flow, she felt connected in the strangest way to all of creation, the earth, the sun, the universe. She was giving life to Gerrod, that which he needed the most to survive. But it was an intense physical pleasure as well, as though the suckling at her neck was connected very low and tugged and teased her as his tongue had done earlier.

Heaven. Pure and simple.

She felt warm and alive and with each draw her heart eased and relaxed and she felt at peace.

Then came something new, a strengthening of the same pleasure but a focusing as well. And now the giving of her sustenance seemed to click into place with her sexuality. Her lower flesh, so tender from the recent orgasm, began to ache all over again. He seemed to know or to understand or maybe he was feeling the same way because his movements quickened. She marveled that he could keep her neck so still while thrusting into her.

It was just pleasure on pleasure as her body gripped him, as the waves of energy caused her fingers to tremble where she slid them over his shoulders and down his arms.

What is this like for you? she asked. But she couldn't imagine that it could possibly be better than what she was experiencing.

Chapter Four

What was this like for him?

Oh, dear Goddess…

Heaven, he pathed.

Yes. Even her voice in his mind teased him mercilessly.

Gerrod was locked into a strange place as he drew Abigail's blood into his mouth and down his throat. He had never tasted an elixir so fine, so fulfilling, so savory of rosemary. He had been a vampire for three-hundred-years, but in all that time, drawing blood had never been so full of a kind of excitement and satisfaction that he couldn't explain.

He lost track of time. He didn't know how long he'd been suckling, but he could tell there was more and more and more. She was an infinite supply, at least she felt like that. Even her blood was a tender sensation in his stomach as though her life filled him now.

His hips pistoned. He was hard and every thrust vibrated against his skin. His balls were tight. He was ready to release, but he didn't want to, he didn't want the moment to end, he didn't want to stop drinking from her.

Abigail had been right about one thing, he'd been a starved vampire for a long time. He hadn't taken his fill in too many years to remember.

He breathed hard through his nose. He held her pinned to his chest and to the bed so that while his cock stroked her deep, he could keep his mouth fixed right over the fang-bites.

Gerrod, this is heaven.

He loved that she could reach his telepathic frequency. *I know*, he returned.

I want to come again, but I don't. I wish this could last forever.

He couldn't have agreed more. But it was time, especially since he'd lost track of how much he'd taken from her. *I'll stop drinking now.*

He didn't want to. He didn't want to stop. But he slowed his hips and thrusts and released the seal of his lips. He examined her neck and was startled to watch the holes close up almost immediately and for the redness to simply disappear.

He knew from a lot of experience to wipe his mouth before he did what he desired more than anything to do next. After he'd pulled the sheet from its moorings and cleaned his face, he rose up over her. "Am I presentable?"

She lifted her brows. "Oh, you mean do you have my blood on your chin or lips? Not much that I can detect."

"Good. It can be distressing if you're not used to it."

Her expression softened and she lifted a hand to his face, caressing him. He leaned into her palm and kissed her.

"You are so thoughtful," she said.

He leaned down and kissed her, savoring her swollen lips, the taste of her mouth, how she moaned as he thrust his tongue. He loved kissing her.

Oh, that vibrating tongue. My, God.

He drew back, then rolled his hips and she arched her back, just as he knew she would. She was right with him, caught in the same level of pleasure. Even where his pelvis touched hers, his skin vibrated against hers.

He knew exactly what he wanted to do and he began a slow steady drive, his cock vibrating deep inside her. He held her gaze as she planted her hands on his shoulders. She tried to match his thrusts but he said, "Allow me." Then he smiled.

She lifted her brows but settled back against the sheet and let him do the work. He began to increase his speed and when she finally understood his intention, she said, "Oh, Gerrod, this is going to feel very good."

He nodded. He even smiled again.

He went faster. He held back, something he could do because he'd lived as long as he had. All those realm-based waves of energy strengthened the faster he thrust into her.

She arched and panted now, right on the edge again.

Gerrod, oh, God, oh, God. He felt her body gripping and tugging at him, preparing. She was very wet and each thrust was a smooth glide in and out of her.

Faster.

Faster.

She thrashed her head back and forth now.

Then he gave her the real treat and sped up so that he moved as only a vampire could move, with a lightning speed that stroked her just right.

She came screaming again, the vibrations nearly a roar now through his body. He couldn't hold back any longer. He began to release into her, pleasure streaking the length of his cock again and again as he came. Ecstasy had a new meaning. He looked down at her, watching her writhe, and still he came, as though he could pump into her forever.

Finally, he began to ease back and slow his rhythm. His breathing was labored and bit by bit his hips relaxed.

A few moments later she began to settle as well, and her eyes didn't roll around quite so much.

So good, her voice drifted through his head.

Yes.

He collapsed on her, staying inside her and rubbing his hands over her arms. She moved them stretching straight out. She kissed his neck and face. She kissed his lips and thanked him.

But he recalled that he had lost a sense of how much blood he had taken. So he lifted slightly and looked her over carefully. Her face had a rosy hue, not even a hint of paleness, she just looked well and beautifully used. "Do you feel all right? Are you dizzy at all?"

"You look worried."

"I wasn't certain how long I took from your vein. I just want to make sure you're all right."

She smiled. "My heart feels perfect now." She sighed over and over.

He relaxed then kissed her in return and licked her neck, both sides. He slid his fingers through hers and squeezed both hands at the same time. She wrapped her legs around the backs of his thighs, rubbing up and down, letting her feet glide down his legs then back up.

All the movement felt good to his hyper-sensitive cock, which remained half erect and content in the depth of her well. His heart reached for her, longing for her to stay in his bed forever.

If only she could, but he knew better. For now, however, he would savor her soft fair skin, the light rosemary scent of her, the way she continued to sigh and coo in her contentment.

*** *** ***

The next afternoon, Abigail awoke feeling melded to Gerrod's bed. Her eyelids were heavy but not in a bad way. She was just so damn satisfied.

But mostly, the weight in her chest was gone.

She lifted her fingers to her neck, wondering if something of Gerrod's bite remained, but nothing was there. No puncture, swelling, nothing and that made her a little sad. She would have liked a physical reminder of all that had happened last night.

She rolled onto her back and realized that Gerrod wasn't in bed. She lifted up on her elbows and listened. The bathroom was quiet as well as the sitting room.

She was alone.

Even so, desire fluttered over her stomach and raced in little shivers straight down her thighs. She ached in the most wonderful places from all the activity last night.

He'd been *wonderful*, attentive, powerful, controlled. And that speed. She felt her cheeks grow warm and she tingled all over again. Just how loud had she screamed after all?

She looked up at the tall vaulted ceiling. Wood rafters. The walls were stone. Maybe no one had heard her.

Fat chance.

She glanced at the bed, all rumpled covers and the sheets really did need to be laundered, which made her smile.

Then she blushed just thinking about it since the entire castle would know by the laundry alone what had gone on in this room for a few hours last night.

Oh, God, a few hours last night. She'd never known such pleasure, such flat-out excitement. Gerrod's frequency was like having sex spread through every cell of her body, over and over.

But as her mind turned to her other concerns, like her sister in Flagstaff and Elena at the new bakery, she became aware that she ought to be leaving. She had told Gerrod she wouldn't stay, that she would return to Flagstaff because of the Invictus outbreak in his realm. But she was torn. She had a bakery to open in Hollow Tree. Many realm-folk were depending on her and the jobs the bakery would provide.

She pulled the sheet up to her arm pits, sat up, and hugged her knees. She pondered all that had happened on the evening before, the wedding and reception, kissing Gerrod deep in the forest, the Invictus attack, saving the little troll child, and later of course, tending to Gerrod and he to her, and all that tremendous feeling of vibration and waves of energy.

She had told Gerrod this would be one night only, but she didn't want to leave this bed, or his castle, or Merhaine. For reasons she couldn't explain, she loved being here. And it wasn't just that the sex had been mind-blowing and tender and all-around-wonderful. She just liked being here.

She felt at home.

The more she thought about what to do next, and with so much general reluctance to leave this realm, she decided at the very least she had to go to the bakery and talk with Elena. Perhaps the evening would bring more answers about all that was happening to her.

With the decision made, she had only one problem to contend with: She didn't have anything to wear except the evening dress she had worn to the wedding last night. But the castle staff was a warm, friendly lot and no doubt would help her with something to wear, at least until she could decide better whether or not to head back to Flagstaff.

Right now, something deep in her bones told her to stay.

*** *** ***

Gerrod sat at the table in his library, his elbows propped up on the table, his hands clasped together, his thumbs at war.

Damn, he was scowling. He could feel the deep pinch between his brows, that permanent look of his as though he was mad at the world. She had said that to him once, some weeks ago, and even last night she had slid her finger along that groove, trying to work the crease out.

Of course, he had no idea why he was thinking about Abigail right now. He shouldn't be. The sex had been great and her blood… oh, dear Goddess, her blood, like a fine wine with just a hint of rosemary, something he had never tasted in the long expanse of his realm life.

He sucked in a deep breath and sat back in his chair. He needed to make room for a sudden arousal.

Very softly, he whistled the elegant folk song that had played during the ceremony. He glanced at the doorway. How many times had he been whistling this morning? It really wouldn't do. His staff would take notice and whisper and smile behind his back.

He scowled a little more. As if they weren't doing that already.

He'd left his bed, not wanting to leave the woman, the human, that which he shouldn't have been with in the first place. He was drawn to her fiercely, yet repelled because of her parentage, her unfortunate DNA.

Human.

Not realm.

Red hair, fair skin that grew flushed and damp, gentle green eyes. He had kissed her cheek and licked the sweet essence of her.

He wanted more.

He leaned forward again, but this time he put his head in his hands.

Must focus.

Realm in trouble. Invictus might attack again, without warning.

He stood up and withdrew his iPhone from the pocket of his leather pants. He marveled. Here was a phone that could reach between the Realms. Ethan had brought the Nine Realms up to electronic speed. As Mastyr Vampire of the Bergisson Realm, he was the youngest of all the mastyrs, being but thirty years in his mastyr state and only ninety from his birth date. So fucking young. And powerful. Ethan had more raw power than any mastyr Gerrod had ever known.

He thumbed the surface and smiled, a little, just off to the side of his mouth. Oh, Goddess, she had kissed that side last night. He wondered about his half smile. Maybe that meant something.

So many decades of carrying the weight of so many lives on his shoulders, however much he treasured and valued each one, aye that was a load-and-a-half, so half-damn him for his half-a-damn-smile.

He chuckled softly and thumbed the front of the phone.

He heard the ring and drew a deep breath. He turned toward the doorway to his library. Was Abigail awake? Had she felt desolate rising in an empty bed? He had despised the footsteps he took to leave the room.

A strong male voice hit his ear. "Hey, Gerrod. How's it hangin'?"

He looked down at his cock. He was fucking upright.

"Ethan."

"What's groovin', bro."

Gerrod laughed. "Groovin'? Is that how we speak now?"

He could almost see Ethan shrug, one of his favorite gestures. "I'm groovin', but I take it you're not. What's going on in Merhaine? You got Invictus sign?"

Gerrod told him what had happened at the wedding.

"Shit. Shit. Shit."

Yes. Shit. Several of them linked together.

"And at a wedding."

"We didn't lose anyone." He almost told Ethan how Abigail saved the troll child, but he swallowed the words. Abigail needed to leave, not become part of his dialogue, realm-to-realm. "The only one of the Merhaine Guard to engage was Jason. There was Invictus sign in the south, but no battling. Just in the north-central area near my castle. Ethan, this group was different. There were forty of them and they seemed organized."

"That just doesn't make sense. The Invictus function in pairs, and packs of maybe six. Never so many, never with a strategy."

"You have just made all my points, Ethan. Would you come to Merhaine? I think we should discuss the future. We may need to act together more cohesively in the near future."

"You'll never get all nine mastyrs to do it. We're too damn independent and ill-tempered." But he laughed.

Ethan was right. The mastyr vampires of the Nine Realms had talked of a federation for decades, especially since the realm world and human world had collided some three decades ago. Permits traveling either direction were extremely limited, primarily to university professors studying realm-folk, and to the nearest connected towns.

However, the joint meetings usually ended with at least four of the mastyrs brawling. Some of the eastern realm leaders had roguish violent tempers.

So who would head such a federation, how would it operate, how could it benefit so many scattered and diverse lands?

And yet something had to be done. "The poorest population in the south loses realm-folk quite often, especially prostitutes and those addicted to hard substances."

"Drain-and-kills?"

"We're not finding bodies."

Ethan snorted. "You've got a big desert out there in the Southwest, in the human lands of Arizona, New Mexico and the northern reaches of Mexico. That's a lot of place to dump realm-folk."

"Even if that were true, what does that suggest to you?"

"I see what you mean: a higher degree of organization. Have any of your politicos been unhappy with the power structure in

Merhaine, maybe motivated to align with the Invictus, create an army of them?"

At that, Gerrod laughed outright. "You are making a joke, are you not, Ethan? I know of at least seven local dignitaries who come to the top of my head right now and all seven I'd love to whip to the edge of the realm and back."

"Hell if I don't know exactly what you mean. All right. I'll get my ass over there. Give me an hour."

"Thank you. And Ethan?"

"Yeah." He spoke in bark-like words, which also quirked up the side of Gerrod's mouth.

"You've been a good friend and I'm grateful."

"Aw, shit, you'll make me weep like a little girl. See you in a few."

Gerrod thumbed his phone. He pursed his lips and whistled once more. This time he kept on whistling. If his staff stared at him and gossiped more than usual, right now he really didn't care.

*** *** ***

After her shower, Abigail put Gerrod's robe on, holding the sleeve up to her nose. She closed her eyes, shivering.

The fabric smelled rich, warm, erotic, that lovely fresh rain scent of his that simply undid her.

Who knew vampires smelled so good?

Opening her eyes, she crossed to the pegs where her gown still hung and checked her thong. It was fully dry.

Now that she was up and moving, her thoughts turned to the bakery, which she and her Merhaine elf partner had dubbed, *Just Two Sweet!* They both thought it was an awesome play on words.

So now there would be *Just Too Sweet!*

And *Just Two Sweet!*

Suh-weeet.

She moved across the bedroom and through the sitting room to the door. The castle was a little old-fashioned and still made use of a well-functioning bell-pull system.

She crossed the room and gave a tug.

A few minutes later, Gus arrived. She was still sunk in Gerrod's massive terry robe, well-covered when he knocked.

The troll stood in the doorway, grinning at her and didn't look like he was going to stop anytime soon.

"What gives?" she asked, but oh, her cheeks were hot now.

His eyes twinkled as his grin broadened. "The mastyr is whistling this morning. He looks well, even healthy."

Her hand flew to her throat. Now her cheeks flamed.

It had all seemed so natural, so exciting, so adventurous last night, but right now she wanted to die. And like hell Gus wasn't sharing all this information with the entire staff of twenty mixed specie realm-folk.

Oh. God.

"Nay, Mistress Abigail. Don't have even a gremlin's tit of distress. Tis a great thing you've done, I swear it. You'll have nothing but respect and much appreciation from the castle employees, I promise you."

She forced her color down and decided she'd have to get used to this unless she wanted to sneak out the side door and hightail it back to Flagstaff.

It was a thought.

But she'd already made her decision. She was going to the

Merhaine bakery. The grand opening had already been announced in the Merhaine Star and the Mayor of Hollow Tree would be on hand to sprinkle the ceremonial herbs. At least three babies had been promised as well, to bring an element of luck to the doorstep.

She squared her shoulders. "I need some help, Gus." She told him of her plans to stay on for at least another day, which brought an almost angelic light to his face as he shifted back and forth on his feet about a dozen times.

"Whatever you need, Mistress. The castle can get anything for you."

"I don't need very much, just a few toiletries, some clothes. I was hoping one of the fae women in residence could provide me with a shirt, pants, and a pair of sandals." Fae feet were unusually long, but sandals would work.

He glanced down at Abigail's feet. "What size are you?"

"A solid eight."

"Oh, that's too bad. You're in-between trolls and fae. Now if we had an elf on staff, but we don't." Generally elves despised any work having to do with home maintenance, a fact of realm life that still didn't make sense to Abigail.

"And I need to borrow a brush and a scrunchy if any of the women have something like that."

"I'll see to it all."

Abigail thought this would take some time so she spent the next few minutes snooping in Gerrod's closet. Of course more of that fresh rain scent poured over her when she pushed the folding doors aside. She found that nearly everything he wore was some version of his Guard battle gear. He had at least a dozen pairs of black leather pants, and a variety of long, sleeveless black leather coats. Gus had once told her that some mastyrs, like Ethan of Bergisson Realm, often wore blue jeans, but Gerrod was much older and continued to sport a more formal, conservative look. The shirts were all made of soft woven fabric died in earth-shades from ochre to maroon to deep blue-green.

He had several pairs of boots as well, but all were similar in design with only a few silver accents to change the overall effect. Rather like corporate men and their suits.

When she heard a knock on the door, her thoughts went straight back to Gerrod.

She hurried over, trying to still her ridiculously beating heart.

She opened the door.

Not Gerrod.

Something second-best, however, waited for her: Gus with a tray of coffee, cinnamon raisin bread and scrambled eggs. "You are spoiling me, my friend."

But he merely grinned at her once more, set the tray on the dresser, and said, "The least we could do for you, mistress." He then waved a fae woman forward who bore a pile of clothes in her arms and several pairs of flip-flops dangling from her fingers.

He then gestured with a sweep of his arm toward her. "Will this do?"

"So much to choose from. How generous you all are. Thank you so much…for everything. Just, everything."

Gus motioned for the woman to lay out the items on the bed and to place the flip-flops on the floor. She then handed Abigail a brush and the requested scrunchy, bowed slightly and left.

Her hair wasn't always manageable, having a slightly unruly curl. But a ponytail would always work in an emergency, like now.

After the fae was gone, Abigail turned to Gus. "Really, my friend, thank you for everything, especially your wise words last night and for showing me the viewing room. I'll never forget this as long as I live." Because her heart was full, she hugged him.

He removed himself from her quick embrace with another rapid shuffling of feet, his eyes sparkling, his color high.

"Oh, mistress, you are too kind." Now he was embarrassed. He hurried from the room.

Note to self: no grabbing and hugging of the castle staff.

Once dressed, Abigail had to steel herself as she left Gerrod's private suite and passed from room to room. She was pretty sure that the entire staff had somehow made it their business to catch sight of her as she made her way to the north entrance, where the driver waited to take her to Hollow Tree. She had never seen so many about sweeping the floor, polishing candelabra, dusting already pristine tables.

She received more old-fashioned curtsies and grins than she had expected, which brought new heat to her cheeks.

Once in the car, she finally relaxed and took a deep breath until the driver said, "Good morning, mistress. It was lovely to hear the mastyr whistling. Very lovely indeed. Indeed."

*** *** ***

"Well, I'll be damned," Ethan said. "You got laid."

Gerrod frowned. He had no intention of discussing Abigail with Ethan. The vampire had a wagging tongue nearly as long as Gus's.

"Thank you for coming."

"Just glad *you came*." He moved into the room in that lethal manner of his. Ethan was an inch taller than Gerrod, with an equivalent larger mass of muscle. He was not a vampire to meet in a blind alley, at least not without a few blade-like or preternatural powers fully in hand.

"I value Augustus tremendously, but he should learn some restraint."

Ethan drew his brow into a knot. "What the hell does Gus have to do with anything? Oh, I see what it is. You think your gossipy troll spilled the beans. Not so, my friend. I can see by your stature you got well and truly fucked last night. Anyone I know, or need to know?" He waggled his brows.

With these words, a very odd tightening began deep in Gerrod's gut. His hands became fists, his biceps flexing before he understood what was happening. "You are not to trouble Mistress Abigail."

Ethan immediately threw up both hands in the surrender position. "Whoa. Didn't mean to give offense. I take it she's someone special."

"No." Too quick at that answer. But to say, 'yes, she is special', what would that mean?

He looked away from Ethan, glancing at the map of the Nine Realms laid out on his table and held at each corner by the most absurd cast iron scorpion weights. Abigail had given them to him for his birthday last month, a peculiar human tradition of giving gifts on the anniversaries of the day of one's birth.

"What's going on, Gerrod? I wouldn't have teased you, been so indiscreet, if I'd thought it serious. Is it? Or is it something else?" Ethan moved to stand on the other side of the massive table facing him.

"The woman is human," he said, though it only covered maybe a tenth of his present concerns.

"Holy shit, you hooked up with a…human?" He crossed his arms over his chest.

Gerrod met his gaze and nodded. Ethan's hair was in disarray. He had a mass of honey-brown curls that always escaped the woven clasps that male vampires used to hold back their long hair. Since the females of his staff tended to hang near multiple doorways when Ethan was around, he was certain that the easy look had a certain appeal.

Besides, the man was a handsome devil, big smile, big teeth, and a certain way of fixing his stare that could unnerve other males and weaken the knees of the females.

But all Gerrod saw was the concern of friendship, and for that he valued Ethan more than any of the other mastyr vampires. For all his relative youth, Ethan could be trusted, counted on.

"I don't want to speak of Abigail at this time. I'm encouraging her to go back to Flagstaff where she lives and not to return."

"Is she with one of the universities that she was allowed to be here in the first place?"

"No. She's opening a bakery in Hollow Tree with an elven partner."

"A bakery? Well that makes sense, I mean, the trolls and fae think sugar was provided by the Goddess herself."

"Yes." He smiled a little.

He grinned. "So, Gerrod of Merhaine in love with a baker." He smiled then laughed, especially since Gerrod had balled up his hands once more.

Ethan sat down in the tall-backed chair opposite and chuckled.

"I won't tease you again. Now, tell me once more about the Invictus attack and just what you have in mind."

Gerrod replayed the incident over in his mind, ignoring the parts that involved Abigail so thoroughly, although he did mention that she helped save the troll boy.

"How?"

"She pathed the need for me to extend my power and cover them."

Ethan squeezed his eyes shut and shook his head back and forth. When his eyes popped open, he said, "Uh, say what?"

"Yes," Gerrod mused. "Abigail, though human, is telepathic. And she can attach my personal frequency."

One brow rose, but no smile this time. "Gerrod, do I need to point out the obvious?"

Gerrod sighed, but he could feel his scowl deepening "The answer is that I don't know what she is, or why a human would have these capabilities. Maybe she's the missing link."

"The creature that connects our DNA to humans."

"Yes. I've wondered."

"All right. Setting that aside, and that you have a conundrum to solve in this human female, I want to know more about what you saw with these Invictus, beyond the numbers and organization."

"The organization is what concerns me. Their movements were more coordinated, attacking from different directions at once."

"But no match for you."

"It was more difficult. I got nicked a few times and one blade grazed my arm, leaving blood on my coat and leathers. That's never happened before."

"Shit. So, in some sense, this could have been a test run."

"A test against me? Perhaps it was. Perhaps against all mastyrs."

"I've never known the Invictus to be so intent on a single goal. What do you think is behind it?"

"An organizing force or person. Be wary, my friend. If someone has chosen to mobilize the Invictus, and also found a way to get them to work together, then Bergisson and all the realms could be at risk as well." Ethan was the Mastyr Vampire of Bergisson Realm that opened onto a northern Louisiana city, in the same way that Merhaine had an access point at Flagstaff in Arizona.

Ethan's mouth grew tight. "We've had increased activity in the west, which as you know is the location of the wastelands of our realm."

Gerrod leaned forward. "Have you noticed a disappearance of realm-folk, of all species, but poorer, some who serve as prostitutes?"

"Not sure. The Guards in the south have been scratching their heads. I'll ask for better stats."

"There, you see. Some stealth is involved. This is not typical Invictus behavior."

"You must be right."

A knock sounded and Gus stepped into the room, his shoulders shifted forward. "Sorry to disturb, mastyrs, but there is a disturbance at *Just Two Sweet*?"

Gerrod leaned back and shifted in Gus's direction. "In Flagstaff?"

"No, that would be *Just Too Sweet!*, T-double-oh. This is *Two Sweet*, as in the number two."

Gerrod smiled. It was a little play on words, but a good one he thought.

"There it is," Ethan said. "You're smiling. I've known you a long time and I don't think I've ever seen you smile."

Words, of course, that brought his brow dropping low once more so that he scowled all over again. "So tell us, Augustus, what is happening at *Just Two Sweet*."

"Apparently, Mistress Abigail has been yelling at the Merhaine press about the rights of all species to be free, in any realm, to conduct business however they believe they should desire to, or something like that."

"Are you telling me she didn't return to Flagstaff?" Hope, his enemy now, blossomed in his chest. She was still in Merhaine.

"Yes, mastyr."

"Oh, dear Goddess."

Ethan grinned. "If she gets the press worked up, she'll start a fucking riot. Does she know women barely have the vote here?"

"I haven't said anything. I suggest if you choose to come with me, you'll keep your tongue as well."

But Ethan merely laughed, not the most hopeful sound.

The next few minutes were spent getting the car and one taunting vampire organized enough to take to the road.

Fifteen minutes later, and within twenty yards of the bakery, Gerrod had his driver stop the car. He saw Abigail across the street from the bakery, confronting a crowd of reporters. Something inside him twisted into a knot and held fast. She looked so different, yet the same, and absurdly wonderful.

She wore a tank top in purple, a light green sweater that barely reached her waist, and jeans. On her feet were flip-flops, much too large. Her hair was in a ponytail and the absence of makeup made her look much younger than last night.

Still this more youthful look made him want to jump from the car and haul her to safety even though he knew she wasn't in any real danger. The press could be obnoxious but never abusive.

His heart started pounding as though it knew what it wanted and his personal frequency began a dreadful kind of wail that he hadn't felt before or was he hearing it?

This is ridiculous.

As he looked her up and down, however, he realized she must have borrowed clothes from his staff. Somehow that made her more real in his life and his heart set up a new kind of racket.

How calm she appeared, gesturing to the crowd of reporters with her hands. Her back was straight although her neck arched forward.

Ethan rolled down the window. "I can't hear what she's saying but the tone of her voice sounds very passionate."

Gerrod had grown single-minded and had only one real thought, that she had been very passionate last night.

And he wished like hell he could do it all over again.

Chapter Five

"Are you dating the Mastyr of Merhaine?" one of the reporters called out.

This question, which Abigail decided would be the last of the interview, startled her and apparently everyone else because the crowd fell silent. She thought of Augustus and his trollish, efficient, but very gossipy self. Had the news spread so fast about events last night?

Evening had descended but at least two stands of bright floodlights kept her blinking.

"Am I dating the Master of Merhaine?" she asked. "I don't see what that has to do with my rights to open the bakery in Hollow Tree, a business that the good City Council approved with a vote of five-to-two? If you have complaints, you should seek out the council members, not me or my wonderful business partner, Elena Goshanne. And now, we have some invoices to review."

She turned her back on the crowd of microphones and

reporters and flashing cameras. Really, the news in Merhaine must be thin today if the press corps had turned out to hassle two women intent on selling cupcakes to realm-folk. Surely, all these reporters should be doing some heavy investigative work on the latest Invictus attack.

She watched for traffic and when she saw an opening, she started to cross. She glanced up the street and recognized a castle car in the distance, a big black car, a car meant to hold Guard-size bodies. Her heart added a few extra beats, but she kept walking. If Gerrod was in there, she didn't want the press to know. That they had even asked about whether or not she was 'dating' him, couldn't be a good thing. What a rumor-mill Merhaine was, feeding , nay feasting on every morsel of gossip however insignificant.

She went inside the shop. It was modeled on the one in Flagstaff, just bigger since there were a lot of sweet-tooths in the realm panting for *Just Two Sweet!* to open.

Two dozen round tables in stainless steel were scattered at the front of the shop, then wrapped around to the right side of the bakery. The far right wall housed a long row of red booths. At each table were stainless steel chairs and red leather upholstered seats, both types of seating comfortable yet not necessarily designed to keep anyone talking for hours.

The bakery was not a coffee shop but had a self-serve counter for baked goods and another bar for coffee and tea. All the baking would be done by a well-trained staff in the back behind stainless steel swinging doors, everything to code. Yep, there was even 'code' in Merhaine.

Of course larger orders would be handled separately.

She didn't find Elena at first, but eventually tracked her down in the storeroom sitting on the floor. "What's going on?"

Elena put her hand to her chest. "I…I don't like having the reporters shouting like that."

Abigail shrugged. "They have to shout because it's their job to get the story. If they don't, the managers of the Times, or the Merhaine Star, or the Hollow County Enquirer will fire them."

"You must do this a lot then."

Abigail laughed. "Never. When we announced the grand opening of *Just Too Sweet*, we had thirty of our friends show up, half a dozen people from off the street, and not a single reporter in sight. No, this is all about me being human. You know it is."

"I suppose so."

Elena tugged at her right ear, then slipped her finger up the outer groove all the way into the narrow, pointed cap. She was an elf, and had elegant ears which she had pierced a couple of times. Tiny stars dangled from silver loops.

Abigail could see she was distressed, so she sat down beside her on the floor of the storeroom and took her hand. Of all the realm-folk, the elven population was more equivalent in size to humans, contrary to earth-based myths. And fae and elves, while similar, had distinct, separate DNA.

"Please don't worry so much, Elena. I promise I'll stay in the back and just do the baking and decorating, or at least I'll keep after the staff to get everything done." Abigail had learned this much about herself, that she enjoyed management more than the actual baking. Though Megan loved to bake, Abigail was much happier checking invoices, tallying up the day's sales, talking with the staff about scheduling problems, all basic management issues for a small business.

She'd even begun thinking of creating a franchise set-up, not because of the baked goods, but because the idea of expansion really appealed to her.

Elena smiled. "For someone who has a bakery, I think it odd that you don't love all the baking and decorating, which I find to be very enjoyable."

Abigail shrugged. "I like it well enough. But the truth is I opened *Just Too Sweet!* for my sister. She was very sickly for a long time, though she's doing much better now, but she did like to bake. We set up a workstation for her that had a variety of stools and every electrical appliance available on the market so she wouldn't have to exert herself."

"What was wrong with her?"

"Bad lungs, asthma. But she's gotten better. She even has two children now and a good husband, of course."

"Yet you worry about her still?"

She glanced at Elena. "I suppose I do. She's been my responsibility ever since I can remember. Even before our parents died, my mother would say, 'You're older. You need to take care of your little sister.'"

Elena laughed. "My mother used to tell me the same thing."

"It's universal. Can't escape it."

She heard the front door jingle.

"I like that sound," Elena said.

"You'll learn to love it once we open. It means customers. That's probably another delivery." She turned toward the door slightly and called out, "Back here."

She stayed put and continued to hold Elena's hand.

The swinging steel doors parted, but instead of delivery

personnel, two large vampires walked through.

Each wore the traditional Guard uniforms of soft draped woven shirts, Gerrod in burgundy, the other vampire, who looked really familiar, in a deep mossy green. Topping it all were the traditional sleeveless, long, sexy-as-hell, coats, which she knew from the forest embrace was made of the softest buttery leather. Shoulder straps drew attention to broad shoulders and expansive chests. The pants were the sexiest black leather. The unknown vampire had his leathers all studded down the sides with large silver medallions.

Her gaze fell to the boots. She had unbuckled Gerrod's for him last night, which was the only thing she could think as her gaze drifted back up to his absurdly handsome face.

She blinked and her heart flipped over a couple of times.

She hadn't seen Gerrod since they'd shared a bed most of the day.

The other vampire spoke. "Well, hello ladies. What's goin' on in here? Havin' a little sit down? A little party, maybe? Need some company?"

Abigail shifted her gaze to the other vampire then she got it: Mastyr Ethan of Bergisson Realm. His smile broadened to reveal a set of big handsome teeth. What a flirt. But she liked his smile so she smiled back.

"Just gabbin.'" She jumped to her feet. Elena followed, but Abigail could sense that her business partner was very nervous. And why wouldn't she be? She doubted Elena had ever been in the company of two mastyrs before.

Gerrod introduced his companion, "Mastyr Ethan of Bergisson Realm."

"Nice to meet you," Abigail said. She thrust out her hand and Ethan took it, but what followed opened her eyes wide. She could feel his vibration, just as she had Gerrod's. "Oh, my God."

Ethan, on the other hand, drew a little closer. "What the hell is that? Are you—"

But he got no further.

Gerrod moved with lightning speed, breaking the connection by putting his massive body in front of Abigail, facing away from her. He then muscled her backwards into the storeroom.

"Hey," she called out. She even shoved at his back but it was like trying to push a concrete wall out of the way.

She glanced at Elena who had decided the farthest corner of the supply closet was a really good idea.

She tilted to get a look at Mastyr Ethan to see what he was doing. But he held up his hands like he was under arrest and Gerrod was holding a gun on him.

"I didn't mean anything by it, Gerrod. She offered her hand and we both know it's a polite *human* thing to take a hand and shake it. I just didn't expect for her to access my personal frequency. See, I'm stepping away." He started backing up. "In fact, I'm going in the other room, and then all the way outside. Yep, I'm going outside."

She put her hand on Gerrod's back and suddenly what had seemed so simple, like yelling at him for being rude, just wasn't. He was trembling from head to foot, like the plague had gotten hold of him in the past few seconds. She could feel heat flowing from him.

She looked back at Elena whose elf eyes were about the size of saucers. Abigail jerked her head in the direction of the bakery proper and Elena shot out of the storeroom like she'd been fired from a cannon.

When Abigail was alone with Gerrod and without removing her hand from him, she moved beside him then in front of him. He was sweating badly and his fangs were heavy on his lips.

"Oh, God," she murmured.

Suddenly her heart pounded. She felt her blood swirling through her veins and now her blood was all lumpish again. Why was she so responsive to this absurd vampire? It almost felt as though she was making all this extra blood just for him. But that was ridiculous.

She wasn't sure exactly what she needed to do right now, but at the very least she was pretty sure that what was going to happen next ought to be private. She closed the door behind her and stretched out her neck at just the right angle. "Are those just for show, or are you prepared to do something with those two sharp points?"

The sound he made was beyond description, like a gargled roar and shout combined. He grabbed her shoulders and with one hand caught the back of her head, holding her immobile.

He licked her neck in long slow swipes, gargling his growl a little more. He wasn't real right now, he was a beast, and his frequency had begun to pound on her, punching at her body so that soon she was limp and that's when he struck, when he felt her whole body surrender.

She felt the hard length of him against her. He drank and drank and with each sucking down of her blood, her heart grew easier and happier, lighter, more fluid.

At the same time, her need for him rose, to have all that beautiful mass that had pleasured her just a few hours ago, inside her once more. She shifted her hand slightly and as soon as he felt what she was doing he created just enough space that she could glide her hand down the front of his leathers.

She found him and rubbed, then groaned. An ache grew, deep inside. Her body responded with deep pulls as though trying to draw within what was held away from her.

He released her neck, but his growls remained.

Off, his mind cried. *Now.*

She wasn't going to pretend she didn't understand. The vampire had a plan and her body was so on board. She lost her jeans and her thong.

With a speed that became a blur of movement, he got his boots and pants off. She gave a little cry as he grabbed her by the waist and lifted her up into the air, then planted her against the door. Good thing the storeroom door was made of solid wood.

She wrapped her legs around him as he slid one large hand to cup her buttocks and tilt her hips. He was chuffing against her neck as he pressed against her entrance, then pushed inside.

She groaned long and loud and hoped to hell Elena had had the good sense to leave the building along with Ethan.

"Can't….help…this," he whispered against her ear. Then he was pumping hard.

"Can't…help…loving…this," she responded. She giggled then cooed then groaned as the vampire settled into a brisk rhythm, his frequency showering her body head to foot as though touching her with a thousand fingertips all at the same time. Without meaning to, she was suddenly shouting at the ceiling, her head arched, as Gerrod slammed into her, all that movement making a drum out of the door. But the orgasm rolled, tugging at her and pulling and swirling, so she kept on shouting.

As he came, his roar filled the small space and for a moment she went deaf. She felt the jerks of his cock, as his rhythm changed then slowed.

He was panting hard.

Her breathing had the sound of bellows.

She looked up at him. His eyes were closed. He seemed dazed.

She was dazed. Stunned, her lips parted. Her mind seemed a little mushy. She felt certain what she had just done with him wasn't a good idea, but her rational mind refused to give her even one reason as to why that might be. Or maybe it was because all the pleasure flowing through her veins wasn't allowing her brain to function at all.

Yeah, that was more like it.

When he opened his eyes, he stared into hers. She stared back. Maybe she blinked. She wasn't sure.

"Oh, Gerrod," she murmured. Then she leaned up and kissed him. He seemed hesitant, almost reluctant, then his arms slipped fully around her and he returned the kiss, sinking his tongue deep.

Heaven, she pathed. *Just heaven.*

Yesssss, returned to her, almost a soft breeze through her mind, a pleasant sensation, so new, yet familiar as though she'd waited for telepathy her entire life.

Oh, good God in heaven. Was she tumbling in love with a vampire?

After a few minutes of more kissing, he pulled out of her and lowered her so that her feet touched the floor.

"Abigail, I'm so sorry. I don't know what happened. Dear Goddess, I was completely out of control." He put a hand over his face.

She caught his hand and pulled it down, holding it pressed to her heart. "It's okay. I was with you all the way. One hundred percent. A willing participant."

"But, it's not okay."

"Well, one thing is for sure, you can't keep doing that. I mean, all Ethan did was take my hand."

"It wasn't that. You tapped his frequency. I could feel it."

"That's right, I did. It was so weird."

But his body stiffened all over again and he had to work to calm down. "Apparently, there's more going on here, more than I comprehend. Just…don't ever touch another mastyr vampire again."

"You think this would be true of all mastyr vampires?"

"Even the thought of it torments me."

She shook her head. "I'm just trying to understand."

He nodded. "Very well, my instincts tell me that you could reach the personal energy of any master vampire."

"Well, then I don't think it'll be a problem since there are so few of you. And because it bothers you, of course I won't touch Ethan again. I promise. Or any others."

He appeared stunned, his eyes wide. "Just like that, without argument?"

She smiled. "I may be pricklish about many things, but I've been in Merhaine for over a year now and I've come to understand that there are differences between my specie and yours. I notice that most men don't draw close to women who don't belong to them, usually at a pace of five feet. I think this was my fault, but I just liked his smile."

"Because I don't smile," he said, scowling.

She couldn't help it. She laughed then launched herself against his chest and slung her arms around his waist, which turned out to be a lot of leather coat to hold even though so soft. But the whole thing was absurd. She still wore her tank top and bra, but had nothing on below. And she had her face pressed against the silver-studded Guard belt.

She liked the feel of his bare legs against hers, though. But man, had her life really gotten bizarre.

He was tentative, but after a moment he surrounded her with his arms as well. Which made her sad because this was his truth, that he hadn't had someone in his life for a long time.

"Don't be ridiculous," she said. "I've grown very fond of your scowl. I may tease you about it but I've come to understand that it reflects how serious you take your job as the Mastyr of Merhaine. I really do understand, or at least I try to. I think that was what I saw when I observed you and the community leaders last night through the entrance hall landscape."

"Indeed? You saw my concern for my realm-folk?"

"The weight you carry on your shoulders."

"Is that why you…washed my hair?"

She looked up then kissed him again. "I washed your hair because I admire and respect the hell out of you."

At that, his scowl softened at least a little and he kissed her back. "You warm my heart."

"Oh. That is the sweetest thing you could have said."

He looked away from her, and his scowl deepened once more. "We need to visit Vojalie."

At that, she backed away from him, feeling her own brows high on her forehead. "I've never met her before. I've heard of her of course. She's said to be the most powerful fae in Merhaine."

"She is. Perhaps in all the Nine Realms. She's also very wise. But I think we need to understand better what is going on here. With you."

"And with us?"

"Yes. I want to understand why I could have killed Ethan right now for touching you."

Abigail nodded. "Well, give me a few minutes, to, uh, make myself presentable."

He smiled. Well, perhaps just a half smile. But it was all she needed.

*** *** ***

Gerrod worked himself back into his leathers and boots, then left the absurd storage room to give Abigail some privacy. He rolled his eyes, all accusatory thoughts leveled at himself.

He had been badly lacking in control. But he had spoken truly when he said he could have killed Ethan and was glad that his good friend and fellow mastyr had understood his dilemma so quickly. If he hadn't backed off, Gerrod would have fought him.

Not a good thing.

How had his life gotten so complicated? He did not understand what was going on. He needed advice, good, worthy, fae advice, the kind he always received from Vojalie.

She was pure fae and wed to a very unattractive troll, whom she adored with every fiber of her being. The union had been one of the most stunning of Gerrod's long life, so unexpected, even absurd, that the elegant, beautiful Vojalie of Shepherd County would have been wooed and won by the homely troll, Davido of

Bergisson Realm.

He was very old, perhaps one of the oldest realm-folk Gerrod had ever known. The best historians thought he was perhaps two-thousand-years-old, but Gerrod had a strange feeling that Davido was well beyond that. Davido seemed to take peculiar enjoyment in refusing to reveal his age. He was funny, charming, and devoted to Vojalie, to her comfort, to her security and protection especially when with child as she was now.

He drew his phone from the pocket of his leathers and made the call.

"Vojalie The Wise's residence, your handsome troll speaking. What might I do for you this fine realm day?"

Gerrod felt his mouth curve up, well at least part of it. "Hallo, Davido. This is Gerrod."

"Well, by the Goddess's beautiful pink nipples, how the hell are you?"

Ethan and Davido got along really well, but then they both had deep ties to Bergisson.

He heard Vojalie in the background. "Stop that nonsense. Give the phone to me. Gerrod's been on my mind for days now."

"Yes, my lovely one, anything you desire." Then to Gerrod, he continued, "Heard you got laid last night."

Gerrod really did need to have a long talk with Gus. Maybe he should seriously think about firing 'his gossipy troll's ass', as Ethan would say.

"I was given a measure of blood by the human and it has bolstered my physical well-being. I wish to bring her to Vojalie to see what she can discern about Mistress Abigail. I," he cleared his throat, "I nearly battled Ethan for her because she shook his hand."

The next words were muffled as though Davido held his hand loosely over the phone, but Gerrod could make out the words. "My dearest most pleasing one, love has struck Gerrod at last. He almost killed Ethan over the human, the one called Abigail."

"Give. Me. The. Phone. You are as bad as Augustus." Gerrod heard a spitting noise.

A muffled 'ouch' followed.

Vojalie did not believe in gossip.

Davido came back on the phone, his voice a few tones higher. "My beloved wishes to speak with you."

Since some loud smacking sounds followed and a little giggling, Gerrod released an impatient sigh. God save him from romantic couples who, after two-hundred-years of marriage, still behaved as though on their fae-moon.

When Vojalie agreed to meet with them shortly, he got off the phone and went outside. Ethan was across the street staring up at the sign above the bakery.

"Clever," he said. He had his hands in his pockets rocking back and forth.

Gerrod drew a deep breath, scowled, and after waiting for a couple of cars to pass, crossed to make amends.

"Ever so sorry, Ethan. My apologies."

Ethan turned and looked at him. First he grinned, then frowned. "So what the fuck's going on here? I mean, don't get me wrong. I'm happy as hell for you. She's…lovely. She's also human and—" He paused, his eyes widening. "Holy shit, the Goddess and her seven Elf-lords…did you just take her blood again? How the hell is that possible? Did you…shit, Gerrod, is she dead? No human, no realm can give that much blood one day following the next."

But since at that moment, Abigail opened the door, smiled and waved, her cheeks still bearing a lovely flush, Ethan's jaw dropped.

"Do you understand now why I must speak with Vojalie?"

"Uh, hell yeah. Who can donate blood like that? I work from a dozen *doneuses* at present and I'm still fucking blood-starved."

Abigail called out, "I just need to speak with Elena, then I'm all yours."

Then she was all his. Why did his chest tighten like that, as though she had spoken an entire volume of poetry?

He waved in return.

"She…she looks healthier than before. What. The. Fuck?"

"I know. Abigail makes no sense at all in our world."

"Unless…"

Gerrod turned to Ethan. "Unless what?"

"I've heard of this thing, it's some kind of rose, but… Aw, hell, never mind. Listen, you've got a lot on your plate right now. I'm heading back to Bergisson. I'll stay in touch. And I'll sure as hell let you know if the Invictus start showing up in bigger numbers or if our realm-folk start disappearing."

"Good. You want a lift?" He gestured to his car.

Ethan smirked. "What the hell for?" He clapped Gerrod on the shoulder, told him to let his hair down with Abigail, then sped off, pathing his way to the Bergisson entry point in the northeast portion of the Merhaine Realm.

Gerrod wondered what 'letting his hair down' with Abigail had to do with anything. Besides, he had already done that last night, which had been extraordinary.

He waited for several cars to pass, as well as a young troll on a bicycle, before he crossed back to the bakery. He glanced up the street and waved his car forward.

By the time Abigail finished up with Elena, the car was ready and he ushered her inside.

The funny thing was, she didn't move to the other side, but instead, sat in the middle and as soon as he shut the door, she grabbed his left arm and wrapped it over her shoulders. She settled against him and sighed.

She was such a strange creature. He looked down at her and after a moment, he allowed his arm to relax and surround her. He even pressed her arm with his hand. He hadn't done this in so long that he had forgotten how to do it, how to be with a woman. He tried not to think how good it felt.

She looked up at him. With his free hand, he cupped her neck and thumbed her jaw. He leaned down and kissed her. He had meant it only to be something soft, without tongue, but before he could even think, he was pushing into her mouth and she writhed against him.

His frequency lit up almost at once, as though it knew Abigail better than his rational mind did.

Oh, God, Gerrod, that wave. It's like magic and so seductive. You could take me again. Right here.

He could. He could do it now. He wanted to push her onto her back and take care of business.

He drew back panting. She stared at him, lips parted, breathing hard. "My God, what you can do to me. Are you sure it isn't some kind of vampire thrall? I mean, *seriously.*"

He chuckled. "Not possible. Doesn't exist. Vampires can't

enthrall." But he kept shaking his head. He'd never been with a woman like this.

Only then did he realize the car wasn't moving.

He glanced at the front seat and saw that his driver was staring forward, quite studiously. Good man. "To Vojalie's."

"Yes, mastyr."

*** *** ***

Abigail had not been to many realm homes, just the castle, Elena's modest cottage and a couple of others. But the outside of Vojalie and Davido's home was a different experience entirely since it was constructed of a series of round structures with what must be long halls connecting the rooms inside.

The carved arched door was made of a beautiful solid dark wood. The carving depicted a woman in flowing robes, who Abigail supposed must be the Goddess, that spiritual being most realm-folk worshipped.

Gerrod lifted the wrought-iron rapper and tapped three times.

When the door opened, her brows rose. Before her was a stately troll who, on the scale of attractiveness, ranked in the lower numbers. She had heard Vojalie was perhaps the most beautiful woman in the realm. Davido had more wrinkles than she'd ever seen on a troll before.

He bowed to her then apologized saying it was a very old habit of his, something from ancient days. "Come in, come in. We are delighted to have you here."

Davido was even shorter than Augustus, perhaps five-three, no more. But he was broad shouldered, and nicely built, his waist narrow. His legs were long and well-muscled for his relative size. He wore a long-sleeved ribbed t-shirt and tailored slacks. On his feet, expensive Italian loafers.

She heard the strangest sound beside her, the softest growl.

She glanced up at Gerrod, eyes wide. *What?*

You were looking at him.

And yes, she was. He took her hand and held it firmly. She wasn't sure what to say. She hadn't meant to stare. *That was rude of me.*

Do you desire him?

Oh, God, no, I'm just surprised sometimes by certain things.

Stop looking at certain things, then.

She glanced back at Davido, who was now grinning. She wondered if he had read their telepathic conversation. But when his gaze dropped to their joined fingers then back to meet her eyes, she understood. The top ridge of his forehead rose slightly as well, a sure sign that his trollish curiosity had been pinged.

Oh, lord, not another gossipy troll.

And yet, there was something about Davido, something almost compelling, as though if he desired he could command her attention for the next several hours. Then she understood. The troll had charisma.

She smiled and offered the smallest shrug of her shoulders. "I'm so glad to be here," she said. "I've heard of the famous Vojalie from the time that I first came to Merhaine."

"She is a delight and a wonder," he said, leaning toward her as though telling secrets. "But you will see for yourself. Please, follow me." He took off down a long hall, wide enough for her to walk beside Gerrod.

The hall was lined with what had to be portraits of her hosts' numerous children, some bearing troll features, some with fae. The DNA lines fell to one side or the other. It made for a beautiful presentation for a home especially since several arched stained glass windows were lit from behind, lighting up portions of the hall in pale lavenders and greens.

The scent of verbena pervaded the space.

But what perhaps surprised her the most was that Gerrod hadn't relinquished her hand, but continued to hold it almost possessively.

She glanced up at him. He was scowling, of course, but in his eye was something more. She realized he was worried. *What is it?*

He glanced down at her. His lips parted, then curved a little, off to one side, but he shook his head.

The hall opened into a place of splendor. She hadn't meant to ignore the fae woman standing on the opposite side of the very round room by the fireplace, but Abigail's gaze was drawn up to the perfectly dome-shaped ceiling. A multi-hued iridescence shone over the entire width and breadth of the dome and moving forward even just a step caused all the colors to change because her position had changed.

"This is so beautiful," she said.

Gerrod squeezed her hand and she glanced at him. He inclined his head in the direction of the fireplace.

Her cheeks warmed again. She turned to the woman, the fae, Vojalie. "I am so sorry, but your home is so beautiful, expressive, warm, magical, so full of love."

"Oh, my dear," Vojalie said, moving toward her slowly, her hands outstretched. "You could have offered me no finer greeting."

Gerrod released her hand. Abigail moved forward to meet the woman and took her hands as though they had been old friends. She felt almost drawn toward Vojalie, perhaps pulled, by the famous magic that a pure faerie could hold.

The fae could enthrall and this one had power that seemed to cloak Vojalie like a garment, an iridescent garment, like the ceiling.

She felt soft waves pulsing from Vojalie's fingertips and once her palms were within Vojalie's warm, soft grasp, she felt she could melt like a big pool of butter right on the stone floor.

How she remained upright she wasn't certain. "Gerrod and Davido, please leave us. I wish to speak with Mistress Abigail alone."

Abigail sort of heard her. She felt as though she'd been wrapped quite thoroughly in a tender web. She didn't think she could move and if Vojalie had been her enemy, she would soon be dead, she was that caught.

She met the woman's soft brown eyes. But the eyes shifted color, warming, lightening until she stared into silver pools, beautiful, elegant, full of light and love. Abigail had the strangest sense she could stay there forever. Was this a spell? Surely a spell.

After a moment, she blinked and the cocoon-like sensation dissipated. "What was that?"

But Vojalie's lips were parted and her eyes were still a silver color as though she was caught in a trance herself. She released Abigail's hands, but the woman remained standing in front of her, still staring at her, but more like *through* her now, as though what Vojalie saw had nothing to do with the present.

One of Vojalie's hands fell to the swell of her stomach. She was tall perhaps five-nine or ten, much taller than her husband. She was a great beauty, just as Abigail had heard. Her rich dark brown hair hung in lovely waves to her waist held back by a narrow headband. The size and luster of her dark eyes, still silver, offset high arched brows. Her nose was narrow and straight, her lips small, her chin tapering to a beautiful fae point, not as severe as the elven women.

"I must sit down." Vojalie turned and made her way to one of the pair of white silk sofas that faced each other and were situated adjacent to the massive fireplace.

Abigail frowned. Something was wrong. She thought about calling Gerrod and Davido back, but Vojalie swept an arm to the couch opposite her. "Please, sit down. I know it must seem like I'm behaving oddly. I suppose I am, it's just that I'm very surprised." She shifted slightly, her right hip pushing out, her belly angling to the left. She planted her left elbow on the back of the sofa and twirled a long lock around her finger. She stared at the fireplace.

She was very pregnant.

Abigail sat with her feet squared up on the floor, acutely aware that she wore only flip-flops and jeans. The woman was dressed in what looked like a layering of three gowns, the bottom layer a vibrant purple silk, then a lavender gauze, overlaid with white gauze.

"I must apologize for my clothing," Abigail said. "I was at the bakery—"

Vojalie whipped her head in direction. "That's right you're opening a bakery. I keep forgetting that you've become a fixture in Merhaine, or at least in Hollow County. I've seen your photo often, most of them candid and all of them unflattering for you are uncommonly lovely, even without make-up. I'm so confused right now." Her gaze drifted up to the ceiling, following the arch the entire distance, the strange iridescence reflected in her eyes, giving her an angelic appearance.

When she met Abigail's gaze once more, she said, "Would you please go to the far side of the room," she waved her hand in the direction behind Abigail, "and fetch that horrible brown leather tome that is about the size of a small wheelbarrow, and bring it to me? I must check something in our history."

Abigail rose and crossed the room quickly. She found the book easily enough and it was enormous. She gripped it in both arms and carried it back to Vojalie. She hesitated putting it on her lap. She looked around. "Why don't I bring the tea cart over."

"Good idea."

She set the book on the sofa cushion beside Vojalie, then fetched the table.

A few minutes later, Vojalie was scowling almost as heavily as Gerrod did normally. She turned to one page, then the next, sometimes using her entire arm to hold her place. She kept going farther and farther back in the book and ended up studying the index and doing more searches. The entire time, she chewed on her lower lip.

Finally, she looked up from the book and met Abigail's gaze. "How is your blood these days? Experiencing anything unusual?"

"You could say that."

Abigail told her everything, that from the time she had started visiting Merhaine, in particular the castle, her blood had grown thick and sluggish because she produced too much and that her doctor occasionally drained away the excess.

Like Gerrod had done the previous day, Vojalie gasped. "What a tragic waste."

"I assure you, it was given to the blood bank."

"Oh, well, that's a relief. Still, not quite the same thing."

"Does this mean something, all this excess blood? My heart feels sluggish until I give it away again." She felt her cheeks warm once more. Her general embarrassment was driving her crazy and yet all of this was so intimate.

"Actually, I believe it does and yet it's a phenomenon that I've only read about. First, however, I'd like to ask you about the Invictus attack, if you are willing."

"Yes, of course."

She smiled, even ruefully. "By now you must be fully aware that my husband, who I adore, is as bad a gossip as Augustus. So much so that I'm persuaded the two of them were separated at birth. So, I know that you were involved with Gerrod on many levels, but if you would, please tell me your version of events."

Abigail related all that she had experienced, even her ability to communicate telepathically with Gerrod.

Vojalie, thankfully, listened carefully without offering comment or criticism. Her countenance was so calm that before long, Abigail had launched into a further explanation of what had happened afterward, at the castle, with Gus, with her own ministrations to Gerrod, the drawing of the bath, washing of his hair. Vojalie nodded, but never smiled, never frowned, just an occasional soft, encouraging nod and the slight twirling of her chestnut hair around her left index finger.

The words poured from Abigail, as though culled magically, and so they must have been.

Without offering too many details of the lovemaking, she even spoke of how Gerrod had taken her blood and that she had experienced Gerrod's frequency.

Vojalie looked so somber afterward, that instead of feeling embarrassed, now Abigail was just plain worried. "I've said too much."

"Be at ease," Vojalie said. "You can be angry with me if you like, but I did use my fae magic. I needed to know everything."

Somehow, Abigail didn't mind, at least not very much. Instead, she experienced a certain measure of relief.

She leaned forward and sighed. "What am I doing here? I don't understand what's happened to me, or why I can do these things. I'm human. I never had such powers or desires before coming to Merhaine." She frowned slightly. "Or before meeting Mastyr Gerrod."

"You seem to have certain markers that once you entered Merhaine came alive, so to speak. It's estimated that at least one percent of the human population could probably experience, at least to a small degree, what you've been going though.

"However, after hearing all you've told me, I believe I now have a summation of events but I'd like to speak with both you and Gerrod at the same time. Will you fetch the men? They are probably by now, deep within Davido's vegetable garden. He's infinitely proud of his creation. No doubt he turned the floodlights on."

Abigail rose to her feet and left by the same set of doors that the men had used earlier. She crossed behind Vojalie and heard the fae sigh very deeply. How bad was this?

Abigail walked the length of the hall, passing by doorways, catching sight of the occasional staff-member performing some household function whether arranging flowers, doing light dusting, or polishing silver since there was a lot of silver in Vojalie's home. Even the kitchens came into view. The chef, an elf about Abigail's height, whisked something pink in a clear glass bowl.

She passed onto a large well-lit covered patio with vines and small purple flowers everywhere. She drew in a soft breath at the sight of the beautiful garden, a rolling lawn, hillocks of trees and flowers here and there, which she could see easily because it was just as Vojalie had said, the floodlights created a near-daylight environment. She saw the path to the back part of the property and could see Gerrod towering above Davido, but bent over examining a plant.

She could have simply pathed him a message, his word for communicating telepathically. Instead, she walked the distance because she was finding it hard to breathe. Maybe it was Vojalie's somber demeanor or the reality that Abigail had some serious realm-like attributes or maybe that last sigh. Whatever the case, it all seemed to pile up on her right now.

When she reached the wall of ivy that separated the garden proper from the vegetable garden, Gerrod turned in her direction. He tilted his head and pathed, *What's wrong.*

She felt strangely close to tears, though she couldn't say why, almost as though she was having a fae moment.

"What's wrong?" he asked, aloud this time.

Davido turned toward her, startled. "*Querida,* what's the matter? How has my lovely wife upset you? I shall have words with her." He moved to her swiftly and took both her hands, just as Vojalie had done earlier.

This time, however, Gerrod didn't react. Perhaps older trolls with very beautiful wives were acceptable to jealous mastyr vampires.

"She said she needs to speak with Gerrod and myself together."

Davido took her arm and turned her back up the path toward the house. "She can be very intense at times."

"I…I don't think that's what's bothering me."

"Then what is it, my child? You may tell me. I shan't breathe a word to anyone."

But at that she laughed. "I have it on good authority that except for a thousand years or so, you and Augustus shared the same womb."

"Ah, my beloved has been speaking badly of me, but if it has made you laugh, then I will not repine. I was showing Gerrod my beans. I have a new variety I'm trying this season. Very green." He talked in that manner so that by the time she returned to her house, she wasn't quite so upset.

However, all that feeling returned when Gerrod sat down beside her opposite Vojalie and he took her hand. She trembled. She couldn't help it. Something life-altering was on the way, she could feel it, the weight of it, even though the words hadn't yet been spoken.

"Sweetheart," Vojalie said, looking up at her husband. "Will you please move the book and table away?"

"Of course, my treasured one." He took care of business, not just setting the tea cart aside but taking both to their proper place. Everything seemed to have a place in Vojalie's home.

He returned to her, but didn't just sit down. He leaned down and took her face in his hands and thumbed her cheeks. He whispered things Abigail couldn't hear, but which made Vojalie sigh then giggle.

Only then did the troll take his place beside Vojalie. He was turned toward her, one of her hands clasped between both of his.

Abigail wondered if this was how those unfortunate people felt who stretched their necks for the guillotine.

Chapter Six

Gerrod wouldn't have been nearly so concerned, except that Abigail was trembling. He could feel her distress, almost palpably, as though she had a personal frequency and was shedding her misery in waves.

Only what on earth had Vojalie said to her that would have caused such anxiety?

So, he waited.

Vojalie leveled her gaze at Gerrod. He stared back.

"I must know one thing," she said.

"Anything," Gerrod responded.

Vojalie smiled, softly but there was a sadness in her eye that now added to his mounting sense of despair. Something was amiss. "I want to know what you are willing to sacrifice for this woman?"

Of all the things she might have said, Gerrod wasn't expecting those words. "What am I willing to sacrifice? In what way? What do you mean?"

"Gerrod, Abigail is a blood rose, even though she's of human stock. I felt it the moment she walked in, but I couldn't believe it."

"I hate to plead ignorance, but in my three hundred years I can't recall hearing about a blood rose." Although, he remembered Ethan saying something about a rose. Maybe this was what he meant.

"I understand. Even I had to examine the ancient documents. There are only a few references of any merit and little help at all. But a blood rose is an individual who can supply a mastyr vampire with an unlimited amount of blood." Gerrod shifted slightly and looked down at Abigail. She looked up, her light green eyes wide. "Sweet Goddess," he murmured.

"Well, that would explain my recurring condition," she said. "And why, after you take what you need, I feel so wonderful." Her lips quirked slightly. "Well, it explains part of the reason I feel so wonderful."

She looked young and adorable and her words teased him mercilessly. *You would say that here, in front of Vojalie and her husband?*

Well, if you heard the questions I was asked earlier, you wouldn't be too surprised. At this point, I think everyone in Merhaine knows that you bonked me last night. As for how soon it becomes known that you shagged me in the bakery closet, well, that will be for Elena and Ethan to reveal.

At that he laughed, bending his neck back, shouting his laughter into the ceiling and it felt good.

"I wonder what she just *pathed* to him," Davido murmured.

"She's good for him."

After a moment, Gerrod's amusement stopped dead as the

harder truths began hitting him. He once more centered his gaze on Vojalie.

"What is the nature of the relationship of the blood rose to the mastyr vampire? Does it involve a ritual bonding ceremony or anything of that nature?"

"Not something specific that I could discover. The bonding occurs naturally over time so proximity would be all that is necessary. Although another brief anecdote indicated that the bond can be hastened by the placing of blood in a receptacle from both mastyr vampire and blood rose, then blending. Once combined, each drinks from the receptacle. Apparently, this can lead to a sudden burst of power, even unusual healing, which I think could be used throughout one's life.

"As for the nature of a blood rose, because she is meant to bond with a mastyr vampire, all mastyr vampires will be drawn to her."

He lifted a hand and said, "Ethan touched her earlier and she immediately tapped his personal frequency."

"The mating frequency?"

"Yes."

"Then you have proved the documents correct. However, there is a remedy. It's important to exchange frequencies during a mating, which then sets a sort of seal on the bond, one that another mastyr vampire cannot cross."

He felt relieved. If Abigail was to be this person, this blood rose in his life, then he had thought it would be very difficult to keep other mastyrs away from her. But a seal, that would be a good thing. His mind reeled from everything he was hearing but he needed to understand all that being a blood rose would mean.

"There must be more."

She nodded. "There is one aspect of the blood rose that might have some application given the recent Invictus activity. For some reason, a blood rose is impervious to the effects of wraith blood, and her blood can even act as an antidote. I believe this means that Abigail would be protected from a wraith pairing should she ever be captured."

Should she ever be captured. The words had a terrible ring to them.

Gerrod pondered all of this. He glanced at Abigail. No smiles right now, just a concern in her eye as she met his gaze.

He turned back to Vojalie. "Can you be more specific about what being a blood rose would mean for Abigail? It is very tempting to think that I might have someone at my side with such an unusual ability. However, it must have ramifications for her."

He watched Vojalie's chest rise and fall before she said, "It does which is why I asked earlier what you would be willing to give up for this woman." Her gaze shifted to Abigail. "I fear your life would change drastically and perhaps not in ways you would wish for. You have come to a crossroads tonight and it won't be simple. If you choose to stay in Merhaine, to live with Gerrod as his blood rose, you will become a vampire."

"What?" the word burst from Abigail like a gunshot. "I don't understand."

"This makes no sense," Gerrod added. "She can't *become* a vampire. No one can. You have to be born one."

But Vojalie extended her hand gesturing in Abigail's direction. "Except, apparently in cases like this."

Once more she shifted to address Abigail. "You're already

half-way down this road or did you think you were born with your telepathic ability and a frequency that even I can sense?"

"I have a frequency?"

"Abigail has a frequency?"

"The beginnings of one, yes."

Gerrod stared at the floor. He was caught between two thoughts that held him suspended over a deep chasm. The first thought was that Abigail could become to him something extraordinary, someone who could provide him with endless blood and who could engage in extraordinary sex because she would possess personaly energy waves. Even dwelling on it this little bit set his own frequency to vibrating strongly. This first how-to-benefit Gerrod musing, however, was pathetically selfish and he knew it.

The second thought was that a human should never have to give up her birthright. He would not wish to cease being a vampire. He'd birthed as one, he was long-lived, he enjoyed all the various aspects of his birth genetics.

So this was why Vojalie had asked him the question, 'What are you to sacrifice for this woman?' If he understood all the nuances, that if Abigail was to hold onto her humanity, he would have to give up hope of ever having her in his life. That would be his sacrifice.

But it was like being offered a gift, even shown the beauty and breadth of that gift, every unique and desirable facet, then having it snatched away. He could feel his scowl return, heavier, deeper than ever before.

He knew only one thing: For a specie to have to change, well it was as wrong as what the Invictus pairs went through. It was a perversion.

He lifted his gaze to Vojalie. "This is a perversion."

He had expected Vojalie to protest. Instead, Abigail spoke quickly. "No," she said, overlaying his arm with her hand. "You're wrong."

Gerrod was surprised at the forceful sound in her voice. "You don't know what you're saying."

"I do know that what I've experienced has felt like a normal progression, something for which I am oddly designed, but I don't believe for a moment it's either immoral or unnatural. I also think Vojalie's concerns are the greater ones anyway."

Gerrod glanced between the two women. "Which concerns?"

Only then did Abigail frown and sink back into the couch cushions. "I will need to choose between the worlds, to determine to which life I will pledge my greater allegiance, my citizenry, my commitment."

And the truth is, she added, pathing to him and looking into his eyes once more, *we barely know each other, the bonking and shagging notwithstanding.*

*** *** ***

Abigail stood in the vast entrance hall of Gerrod's castle.

So she was a blood rose.

Something so uncommon in Realm history that Gerrod had never heard of it and Vojalie had been forced to search through the old leather tome to find out what she could about the strange condition.

The drive back from the fae's house had been very quiet. Silent, in fact.

She had no idea what his thoughts were, but during the entire drive, hers had been an internal, mental round robin of weeping, wailing and screaming.

She wanted to stay with Gerrod in his castle and in his arms forever and yet, did she really? What did she know of him, except that he was a lonely, scowling Guard of the Realm, a mastyr vampire who ruled over a million souls of varying species, an admirable man in essentials, a wonderful lover, a good friend, and very hard on himself.

But could any of this, anything really, justify changing biology.

He stood staring at the stone floor, his hands on his hips, the soft leather coat bunched at the waist.

"What are you thinking?" she asked.

Gerrod turned to face her. She thought it odd that right in this moment he must have been standing in the very center of the massive hall, a large wagon-wheel-like wooden candelabra suspended over his head, though at least some fifteen feet above his tall frame. Was he trying to center himself?

"I honestly do not know what to make of this turn of events. I was looking for an answer more along the lines of, 'Well, Gerrod, I believe this woman to be your mate, even though she is human.' That would have been entirely sufficient. The problems would have been more like whether I could persuade you to live in Merhaine at least part of the year or if you would agree to a bodyguard when you worked at the Hollow Tree bakery.

"But this is so much more. This is impossible. You can't give up your human world. Your connections and involvement with your sister, Megan, alone are paramount."

Abigail sighed heavily. "That you would say as much, makes

this harder still for me."

"How so?"

"Because I value that you understand how important Megan is in my life."

"She's your sister. Of course she's important. And you have a niece and nephew. Because my birth family lives in one of the European Realms, I think of my castle staff in much the same way. I don't think I could be asked to give up Gus, for instance."

"Even with his wide mouth and flappy tongue?"

He smiled just off to one side. Her heart constricted a little more. "He could have a hundred such defects and I would still need him in my home."

"But would I be able to visit Flagstaff, I mean, if I made this change?"

"You would become vampire and how you perceive the world would change. Your frequencies would grow in strength and it could become uncomfortable to visit at times. You would have blood needs. Your life would be very different from Megan's, as different as mine is from yours right now."

And Megan had always relied on her. Always.

But she had a husband now, and yet, it was to Abigail that Megan always turned. When her girls were sick, Abigail had taken shifts caring for them through the night, for several nights in a row.

Besides, Abigail had always seen her Merhaine adventure as just that, a little excitement to while away her days. She just hadn't counted on falling in love with a vampire.

Gerrod moved close and took her hand. "There is something else I want you to think about. This is a dangerous time in our long history because of the rise of the Invictus. The attack last night was different, which indicates an escalation on the part of the enemy, and we don't know the direction the attacks will turn. Ethan said that in his realm, the Invictus have also grown more active in the wastelands. He's checking even now to see if the poorer realm-folk of Bergisson have been disappearing as they have here.

"As for myself, Abigail there is part of me that wants to keep you with me always. I've been half in love with you since that first day, when I caught your very sweet rosemary scent. All that Vojalie's pronouncement meant today is that now I have words for what has happened to me. I've found my blood rose and I want to keep you for so many reasons.

"But I also believe I must let you go. I don't approve of this arrangement. I can't abide the thought that you would give up your heritage. That is a perversion to me even if you say it feels natural and good, nothing forced.

"You should go home. At the very least, go home to think about all of this. And if you don't come back, trust me, with all my heart, I will completely understand."

He looked forlorn, such an old-fashioned word, but that was what he looked like to her, standing there and making his usual Gerrod-like sacrifice, thinking of others rather than himself.

For that reason alone she wanted to stay. Gerrod deserved to have his life eased and there was no question in her mind that she brought exactly that to his life. The fact that he had almost started smiling while she was with him was an indication all by itself.

But he wasn't smiling now.

The trouble was, she couldn't possibly think about making such an enormous decision without talking it over with Megan.

She also had a profound sense that if she left, she would never come back.

This forced her feet to march forward and though he didn't exactly open his arms, she pressed her chest against his, closed her eyes, and slung her arms yet again around his waist.

She held him fast. After a moment, his powerful arms surrounded her as well, tighter this time than ever before.

"Abigail," he said softly. She felt his lips on the top of her head, a tender gesture. That defined him exactly, all this brawn, yet underneath so much tenderness and sacrifice.

What on earth, or even in Merhaine, was she going to do?

*** *** ***

Gerrod sat in his fat leather chair in the entrance hall, feeling like he wanted his bottle of whisky for a while, maybe for the rest of the night.

Abigail was gone.

He'd snapped at three of his staff.

Gus, upon hearing the news of her departure, had lifted his chin, his lips set in a grim disapproving line. "You sent her away?"

"None of your business, troll," he'd growled.

"The Goddess's nipples it's not," he had muttered, heading back to the nether regions. His feet did a strange angry troll march that Gerrod only saw on those occasions when Gus was as mad as fire.

Let them all scowl at him and mutter hard things against his character.

Abigail was gone.

His head fell forward. He planted his elbow on the arm of the chair and with what seemed like monumental effort, supported the weight of his head in his hand.

He felt as though the moment she stepped into his car to go back to Flagstaff, she had sliced his heart from his chest and taken it with her. He had watched from the front of the castle, the door thrown wide. He caught the last glimpse of the car, the last wink of taillights, the last roll of dust and pine needles as the car caught the shoulder then sped down the dark pavement.

Abigail.

He had remained in the doorway, trying to pretend that he would be just fine without her.

Now, as he sat with the door shut on an immediate past that had just cut him off at the knees, he tried to have some perspective. He'd been right to think of her life and her happiness and to send her away. It could never be a bad thing to act in someone else's best interest, surely.

Except that his chest was a vacant hole and already his body was craving a hit of her blood, that elixir flavored with just a touch of rosemary, the taste which had brought his member to proud attention, and which in turn had given her pleasure.

He wished her back. He would swallow all his words of self-sacrifice.

He wished her back a thousand times.

*** *** ***

Abigail returned to Flagstaff and to her home at the end of a long private road. The two-story house, her pride and joy, backed up to the forest. Her two cats had missed her, Frida and Diego, but looked well-fed from a neighbor's cat-loving care.

Could she bring her cats to Merhaine? Could they live in the castle? How would a mastyr vampire feel about a cat box?

She laughed, but the sound came out tinny. She poured Fancy Feast into two separate bowls, and watched her tabby and her tuxedo lower their heads and begin the small familiar bobs of chowing down.

Cats had simple lives.

Hers wasn't.

On the following morning, she called the bakery, but was surprised when a part-time employee, Joy, answered the phone. "Hey, Joy, I didn't think you worked today."

A long pause.

The hairs on the back of her neck stood up. "What's going on?"

"You don't know, do you?"

"Know what?" Oh, God.

"Megan's in the hospital."

Abigail's gaze skittered back and forth over the kitchen island as though hunting for a place to land. "She's in the hospital? When? What happened?" And why hadn't anyone called her?

"Last night, late. But I'm not sure why. Megan said not to bother you, that you had a date in Merhaine."

"Not a date. A wedding."

"Huh. She called it a date. Said it was with some hot uber-hunk."

In the distance, Abigail heard the jangle of the hanging silver doorbells of the bakery. A customer. "I'm heading over to the hospital now."

"Okay. And would you let us know what's going on? We still

haven't heard from Megan or Joe."

"Yes, of course."

She called Megan's husband first. Joe picked up on the second ring, but he spoke quietly. "Hi, Abigail. I'm so sorry. She wouldn't let me call. She didn't want to disturb your date. Everything's okay. No asthma, I promise. It was her appendix. They took it out. She's resting."

Abigail released a very deep breath. "I'm going to get cleaned up and I'll be over in about an hour."

"Sounds good. Really, Abigail, no worries here, I promise."

Abigail hung up then headed upstairs to her bathroom. She stripped, got the water going at just the right temp, then let all that moist warmth beat some of the tension out of her.

Later, at the hospital, Megan lay on her back, her face very white, her red hair splayed out on the pillow. "The drugs are great," she said, but her smile had one corner turned down.

"You were hurting."

"It hurt like a bitch."

"Why didn't you call me?"

"Because I wanted that vampire to see you in your beautiful gown."

He'd seen her all right. Then she'd seen him. *All* of him. She'd even donated blood. She'd learned she was something so rare in realm-lore that Gerrod had never even heard of it before. And she'd seen the Invictus. Oh, God, it all seemed so unreal or at the very least something that had happened years ago and not hours.

Abigail pulled her chair closer to the bed and took one of Megan's hands. "I'm sorry I wasn't here."

"Joe was. You don't have to feel bad. I don't want you to feel bad."

Abigail smiled, but she felt so sad, though she wasn't certain why. "Well, I'm back now. Elena has the bakery well-in-hand in Hollow Tree."

"But you'll go back, right?"

She shook her head. "Not right away. There's quite a bit of objection to a human opening a business in Hollow County. We're going to let the dust settle." It might not have been the complete truth or even a fraction of the truth, but keeping out of sight for a while would not be a bad thing.

"What are you not telling me, sis?"

"Nothing." Much. She sighed. She stared at the light blanket on the bed and on the clip over Megan's finger, monitoring her heart rate.

"Okay. I can see that you're not going to talk, but at least tell me about the wedding. Was it much different than ours?"

*** *** ***

Gerrod shouted up the hall from his private sitting room. "Gus, where the hell are my socks?"

He'd been shouting a lot lately and his scowl was sitting hard these days, low on his brows. Gus told him yesterday he was developing a troll-ridge and that if he wasn't careful he'd be switching species any day now.

His temper was off the charts. Two weeks, two horrible weeks had passed since he'd last seen Abigail at Vojalie's. Sweet Goddess but he was irritable and the blood starvation was back. He needed to call one of his *doneuses*, but the Goddess help him, he couldn't tap the number on his phone.

He blamed Abigail for this, that he'd gotten a taste of rosemary blood and now nothing else would do.

He returned to pace his bedroom. He couldn't find his socks, at least not the kind he needed for his boots. He had to have just the right kind. Gus knew that. What the hell was wrong with his castle staff anyway, that his drawers couldn't be kept full of the socks the Mastyr of Merhaine preferred?

If he had to fight the Invictus now every night and if he had to make sure that one million souls were safe, he should at least have the socks he wanted.

He went to the doorway, and shouted again, "Where are my fucking socks?"

Gus appeared at the top of the hall, the only one that led to his private suite. His expression was grim. He carried a large wicker basket in both hands. His lips had become a thin white line.

"About fucking time." He moved back into his sitting room, stomped into his bedroom, paced in front of the bed. His boots sat there, waiting. Gerrod had Invictus to face tonight again. Did no one understand that his life had become a nightmare?

The bastards had become active as hell and now he cursed as much as Ethan.

Why the hell hadn't Abigail even called him? A simple courtesy call was the very least he had expected. 'No, I can't become a vampire. So sorry.' At the very least she should have called and said that to him.

Goddess, he would kill to hear her voice.

Gus appeared in the doorway, lifted the wicker basket to his shoulder, and with the apparent use of all the strength he possessed, he flung it at Gerrod.

The wicker struck him with all the force of a pillow against his right arm. He batted it away and about a hundred socks flew in every direction, some pink, some purple, many embroidered with flowers, none of them his boot socks. The basket landed upside down near the bathroom. "What the hell? What's going on here. Gus—" His bellows echoed around the stone-walls of the room.

He followed after him and shouted one more time, "Gus, what the fuck was that all about."

Gus did not even turn around. He just flipped him off and kept walking.

*** *** ***

Abigail iced another cupcake.

Megan sat on a chair, bent over, and with artistry and skill, squeezed another leaf from yet another bag of well-crafted green icing. She did the leaves swiftly, one after the other, and they were nearly identical, perfect, and very leaf-like.

She was recovering well and insisted on doing what she could to help with all the orders, especially the ones to Merhaine.

"Joy tells me that you haven't once been here when Gus comes to pick up the cupcake orders."

"I think it's best."

Megan lifted the icing bag from her leaf job. "Are you ever going to tell me the truth about what happened two weeks ago?"

Abigail shrugged. How could she explain the silence that had fallen on her, as though to speak of Merhaine was to make it more real than she could bear. She had made her decision. She couldn't leave Megan. Ever.

Megan set the bag of icing down and rose carefully from her

sitting position. She rounded the long stainless steel worktable, getting in front of Abigail. "Talk."

But Abigail moved away, turning in the direction of the sink. Maybe cleaning up the dishes would help. She flipped the hot water on and thrust her hands into a pair of heavy duty yellow gloves.

She began to rinse and arrange the dishes in the commercial grade dishwasher.

Megan got up close supporting herself with forearms on the counter. "You're in love with him."

"Maybe."

"There's no maybe. Oh, my God, Abigail, are those tears?"

"What of it?"

Megan reached over and shut the water off. "You have got to talk to me."

Abigail couldn't pretend anymore. She slumped to sit on the tile floor, pulling up her knees and balancing her arms right on top of both. Megan eased herself down to sit beside her. "Just so ya know, I won't be able to get up by myself."

Abigail nodded, but she couldn't see much. Everything was a blur behind a wall of unshed tears. "I just have to get over him. I'm sure I can." She rubbed her throat, trying to ease the sudden painful constriction. She remembered the last time Gerrod had sunk his fangs. He'd held her pressed against the storeroom door in the Merhaine bakery.

Then there was nothing but tears, about a million of them.

Megan rubbed her shoulders, her arms, her hands. At some point, she must have struggled to her feet then returned to sit beside her once more because she shoved about a dozen tissues at Abigail. She used every one.

When at last the tears began to subside, and the brokenness of her heart had become more of a drifting kind of pain in her chest instead of a painful strike against a forge, she told Megan everything.

'Oh, my God', fell from Megan's lips about a hundred times.

"So you would become a vampire."

"Apparently I'm almost halfway there as it is."

Megan blinked a couple of times, staring at her hard, her eyes narrowed slightly as though considering everything Abigail had been through. Finally, she said, "You have to go back."

"Don't be ridiculous."

"I'm not. You have to go back to Merhaine."

"But, if I do, I'll want to stay."

"Exactly. I think your heart is already given."

"I can't leave you. I won't."

"Abigail, the truth is, I don't want you to leave Flagstaff either, not if it means you'll never come back as just human. I'd rather keep you here as my big sis, the one I can always turn to no matter what happens, the one who gave me such tremendous security for a good long decade. But I think you need to do this especially since I know you've been unhappy for years now."

"No I haven't," Abigail retorted. "I've enjoyed the bakery and I love your girls. You're my life, Megs."

"That's not what I meant. Let me say it differently. You've never had a choice about your life before. Never. Now you do. And the only question you really need to ask right now is: what do you want?

"I'm not that sickly child anymore and our parents have been gone for a long time. I found the love of my life and I've built a life with him. The bakery, Abigail, well, it was the biggest gift you could have ever given me.

"I'm suited for this work, but the one thing I've come to realize, especially when you got so excited about opening a second bakery in Hollow Tree, is that you're meant for different things, maybe even bigger things." She gestured with a wave of her hand in the direction of the leaves she'd been making. "How many of those have you made?"

"What? The leaves?"

"Yeah, the leaves. How many have you made today?"

"None."

"I've made about a thousand, did you know that?"

Abigail shrugged but she was a little surprised. "Really? Although, given how many cupcakes we sell, and how many leaves go on each one, it makes sense." She laid her head on her knees. "Don't you ever get bored, though?"

"You mean like you?"

"Yeah. Bored like me."

"You've just made my point. I'm never bored. Not even making a thousand leaves a day. *Never.*"

At that, Abigail lifted her head and stared at her sister. "We're very different, you and I."

"Yes, we are." Megan squeezed her arm. "I think you need to look at this situation differently and ask whether or not this new, unexpected path is the right one for you. Joe and I will adjust, so long as the girls get to see their Auntie Abigail every once in a while, fangs or not."

Abigail couldn't believe that Megan was actually giving her permission for something so outrageous. "So you really wouldn't mind if I became a vampire?"

Megan shrugged. "I'll admit it would be strange, and probably would be for awhile, but that's not what matters. I want you to be happy and I want your life to mean something to you. Right now, here in Flagstaff, Abigail this isn't *your* life you're living. It's mine."

All the pieces fell together with those words. This was Megan's life that Abigail helped build for her, with never a thought for herself. But she had meant what she had said. She'd never been unhappy.

But now, for the first time in her life, she could think beyond the bakery, beyond her human life, perhaps even embrace a life lived mostly at night, in the dark, in a castle, beside a wonderful vampire that yes, she had come to love.

"I love him," she said.

"Oh, Abs, even I could see that."

Abigail laughed. "I feel like I just wasted the last two weeks."

"I would take that as an insult since you've been helping me, but in this case, I think I agree with you."

Abigail's heart grew light, as though a tremendous burden had been lifted. She turned to her sister and hugged her, although taking care since she was essentially still recovering from surgery.

"Thank you," Abigail said. "I mean, I have no idea what has happened in the last couple of weeks or even if he wants me. But I'm going to find out."

But even as she had this thought, a vibration passed through her and she had the worst feeling that something had gone wrong in Merhaine.

*** *** ***

With lightning speed above the ground, Gerrod swept past the frontline. He could see the troll family under attack by a wraith in flight circling above like the vulture she was. He was battling deep in Shepherd County, in a rural area, his vampire ability to see at night setting the landscape in a glow. The creature would dive in, and strike, hurting one or the other of the three realm-folk huddled together.

Her partner, a vampire, also moved with astonishing speed, a sure sign they were symbiotic, a joined pair. The perversion of becoming Invictus added tremendous power and unfortunately a seemingly endless desire to do harm to the helpless.

The vampire was less subtle and jerked the husband away from mother and baby. He carried him a hundred yards distant and began to feast. The troll's legs flopped up and down.

Derek pathed, *We see them, Gerrod. Jason's on his way.*

Stay back for orders. Let me get this pair shredded and the family to safety.

He heard the troll baby shrieking and could see that it bore slices on its arms.

Fury tightened Gerrod's chest. He readied his power as he flew in their direction, just a foot off the ground, upright, his hands and arms vibrating, ready to release killing streams of energy.

But just as he detected movement to both his left and his right, he was suddenly somersaulting through the air. His limbs were caught in what he finally recognized as some kind of netting.

With his face smashed into the netting and near the ground, his body upside down, he watched the wraith go in for the kill and finish the family off, shrieking her victory as she then flew in his direction, her eyes dark with blood-lust.

He couldn't move. He couldn't harness his power. And he couldn't telepath his Guards.

What the hell had the Invictus done to him?

Then he smelled it: Fae magic, something done with oils. The netting was covered in it and in a flash, darkness spread over his mind, then nothing.

*** *** ***

Abigail got a strange sick feeling deep in her stomach, a stronger version of what she had felt earlier. She wiped the last of the tables. The hour was past eight and she was ready to close. Bakeries weren't known for evening traffic and the last of the staff had just left. Megan had gone home hours earlier. Both Joe and Abigail had insisted on it.

But Megan had also insisted that she reschedule for the next few days so that Abigail could go back to Merhaine and make her final decision.

Now, as she grabbed her purse and took one look around, her gut tightened a little more.

Abigail.

Her heart twisted into a quick knot. That was Gerrod's voice, so faint, but she was sure of it. Something was wrong, terribly wrong.

She had to get to Merhaine.

She switched the lights off and nearly fell backward because a short figure was on the other side of the door and now knocking in swift jabs on the glass. "Abigail, tis I, Augustus."

She pulled out of her sudden shock, moved to the door, and let Gus in. He danced from foot to foot, clearly upset. Tears coursed down his face. She flipped the lights back on.

"My God, what's the matter? What's happened?" Then she felt it. Somewhere, far away, Gerrod's blood called out to her. "He's blood-starved again, isn't he? But there's something more."

"The Invictus have him."

"What?" She weaved on her feet, but Gus grabbed her arm and kept her from toppling over.

She planted her back against the wall to steady herself. "Tell me everything."

The recital spoke of Gerrod bellowing, growing weak, something about socks, and that the Invictus, the same night that she left Merhaine, had begun attacking various parts of the realm. At least a score of realm-folk were dead and dozens missing, some even from the more prosperous neighborhoods.

"This sounds like war has been declared."

Gus mopped his face with an embroidered handkerchief. "Can you help us?"

"I don't know. I want to, but Gus, what can I possibly do that Gerrod's Guards can't?" But she had to go. Gerrod needed her.

"We can't get through to Mastyr Ethan and no one can pass the boundary to Bergisson Realm."

"Good God."

How frivolous her former concerns became in this moment, as in could she handle becoming a vampire, when Merhaine and its citizens were in so much danger.

Yet, what could she do?

She certainly couldn't face down an entire army of Invictus pairs.

Her heart thumped hard all over again. She could feel her

blood thickening again, really fast, apparently anticipating what needed to be done.

She put her hand on Gus's shoulder. "Take me to the castle and we'll go from there. Okay?"

"I have the car waiting."

"No," she said. "You need to bring one of the Guards here. I know that each of them have nearly Gerrod's level of speed."

"Right. That's the way to think this through."

He got very still. He closed his eyes, sinking into his inter-world telepathy. He jerked forward a couple of times, 'pathing' missteps perhaps.

Finally, he opened his eyes. "Derek will be here in three minutes. He was already at the castle trying to contact Ethan again. But he couldn't get through. Nobody knows how to get Gerrod back."

Abigail made her own phone call. "Hi, Meg."

"What's going on? I know that tone of voice."

"I've got a vampire to save."

She could feel Meg smiling. "Come back to us when you can."

"I will. Take care of my cats?"

"You bet."

When Derek arrived, he had blood smeared over one cheek and on both arms. She withheld a gasp and forced herself to take deep breaths. "I am sorry, Mistress Abigail."

"It doesn't matter. Not even a little."

She turned to Gus. "Thank you for coming to get me. You did the right thing and I'll do what I can to bring him back."

She stepped into Derek, slung her arm around his neck and put her right foot on his left instep. "Take me to the castle. Now."

She buried her face inside his shoulder and his strong Guardsman arm held her tight against him.

A moment later she was air-borne, the wind whipping by her, the smell of the Ponderosa pines sharper because of the speed.

Minutes later, Derek slowed, came to a stop, then cried out, "Oh, shit."

He flung her to the ground to protect her since three wraiths flew in circles in the front yard of the castle. Beneath them three bonded vampires levitated a foot above the ground, all waiting.

But she opened her path to Gerrod and found him. *I'm with Derek. Three wraiths, three vampires. What do they want?*

Oh, dear Goddess.

Gerrod, what do they want? You must tell me.

You. They've come for you. Why did you come back? They can't breach human territory.

I came back for you.

Dear Goddess, no. I didn't want this.

She felt his guilt and knew to prolong the conversation would only create further agony for him. She cut the communication short. Whatever she did next had to be her decision.

She reached out to Derek, pathing toward him and found his telepathic frequency. *You must leave.*

Never. He glanced at her then back, ready to battle the enemy. He had already extended the boundary of his power creating a massive shield in front of her.

"We want the human, Abigail of Flagstaff. She must come with us. If she does not, Mastyr Gerrod will die, within the hour."

"You lie," Derek shouted.

"They're not lying," Abigail said, drawing close to him. "I just pathed with Gerrod. He's close to death, an hour, no more, unless I can get to him and save him."

"You know what they'll want."

She glanced up at the wraiths. *For us to complete a symbiotic Invictus joining.*

Exactly. They might even be able to force it.

If it came to that, she pathed, meeting his gaze fully, *Gerrod and I would die first. For now, I'm his only chance at survival. Please trust in that.*

He stared hard at her, holding his power steady, protecting all the castle inmates, even herself. She could stay here and survive. The wraiths and vampire companions would not dare to challenge him. He could take them all right now and they knew it.

But above all, Derek was sworn to protect his mastyr. The Invictus pairs knew that as well.

"I want to know one thing," he said, addressing the nearest vampire. "How did you know Mistress Abigail would be here tonight."

The wraith closest smiled. Her fangs were very yellow, her lips almost black. "One of our pairs is fae and has foreknowledge of events. This she saw." The wraith flew and waved a hand at Abigail. "Watch what she does. She will move past your power."

"That's not possible."

Oh, but it was. Abigail was half-bonded with Gerrod and felt a knowing deep inside that she could do exactly that.

She pushed past Derek's vast field of power.

Derek kept his power steady but he cried out a powerful, 'no', that echoed through the forest.

Abigail knew what she had to do. She squared her shoulders.

"All right, which one of you bloodsuckers is giving me a lift to the wastelands."

The tallest and most brutish Invictus vampire moved forward, dropping to stand on the ground. His smile revealed another pair of yellowed fangs. Did Invictus vampires always have yellowish fangs like their wraith-mates?

"I am here for you," he said. "And it will be a ride you'll never forget." She really didn't like the sound of that.

When Derek tried to stop her, she turned to him and pathed, *This is our only hope. Protect the castle and I'll do everything I can to bring Gerrod back.*

Derek seemed to settle into himself as he nodded. "Very well."

She slowly put her arm around the Invictus vampire's neck and planted her foot on his left instep. He levitated. She would have buried her head, but he forced it back instead and the next moment, his fangs were buried in her neck and she was moving.

It was a very strange experience to feel the blood leaving her body, and not in a happy way, as she sped through the forest. She had to close her eyes since the sight of the ponderosa canopy whipping by made her nauseous. Or maybe it was the smell of this creature who had hold of her. Or maybe it was that he sucked her blood down with a speed that matched his flying skills.

Before she reached the wastelands, she no longer held onto the vampire. She no longer could. She no longer knew anything.

*** *** ***

Gerrod sat against the brick wall. He could barely hold his head upright. His blood starvation had reached a critical point, that place in vampires that put him on the brink of death, wobbling back and forth.

His vision pared down to the still figure on the floor, her red hair fanned over the uneven gray flagstones. Her back was to him, one arm caught beneath, her hand palm up, fingers motionless.

She breathed in light breaths, high in the chest.

She was dying, almost drained of blood.

The vampire that had dumped her on the concrete floor was in a state of ecstasy. "So much blood," he had said, laughing as he closed the cell door, locked it and headed back up the hall.

So here they were, both dying.

An Invictus wraith had come in earlier to tell him the good news that Abigail had been captured. He'd been too weak to do more than stare at the wraith, horrified. Worse followed when the terms of life for Gerrod and Abigail were established: They were to agree to form a symbiotic pair or be terminated.

"How would we become such a pair?" Gerrod had asked. "I've always understood that a wraith must be part of the pair."

The wraith then explained that for the past hundred years, a very great and wise mastyr vampire, the Great Mastyr as she called him, had been doing experiments with the unique bonding properties of wraith blood. He had also steadily created a deep organization of wraiths, hand-picked for their ability to reason and to follow orders. Hence the recent attacks and the increased number of wraith pairs.

From those experiments, the Great Mastyr had interesting success when he used a human and a vampire. Once their blood was blended in a vessel and a fair amount of wraith blood added, it was as though the couple had become power-bonded like a wraith and a chosen mate. When the Great Mastyr had been informed that the Mastyr of Merhaine himself was dating a human, the rest followed.

Abigail and Gerrod would be the first of many very public experiments.

Gerrod had answered simply, "I would rather die first."

"We hope that isn't your choice."

He remembered thinking there was something odd about this. "Why wouldn't you just force us to do it?"

The wraith rolled her eyes. "For some odd reason unless the couple consents, if the act is done against the will of either, death follows. The Great Mastyr is still working to resolve this issue."

He had one more question, since he had never spoken with an Invictus wraith before. "Why do you kill? What is it in the Invictus bonding that creates such sadism?"

The wraith merely smiled. "Killing in this way provides a tremendous rush of exhilaration and increased power. The symbiotic relationship, in which wraith and servant feed one another in a continuous loop helps sustain that power level. The whole is very addicting and pleasurable."

So here Gerrod was, barely able to keep himself in a sitting position against the wall, with his beloved at his feet, and the only alternative for life that presented itself was becoming a wraith-based couple.

But perhaps what hurt the most was the simple, wonderful fact that Abigail had come for him, even knowing all that had happened, that the Invictus had been making a battlefield out of Merhaine, she had come for him.

He blinked, but it almost hurt to make that much effort. His eyes were wet. So were his cheeks.

The room was an oversized prison cell with a concrete floor and a glaring fluorescent light that buzzed overhead. He turned his head slowly to look out the small window, barred with a steel grate. Why the hell couldn't he have been more like the fictional vampires and been capable of dematerializing? There were a few who could, but his DNA was just that much closer to human than the vanishing-gifted of his world.

He had speed though, but much good that would do him here, locked in a cell, near-death.

He shifted to stare at Abigail. He missed her, he needed her, he loved her. He recalled the moment at the wedding reception when Abigail had poked two fingers into him and said, 'You need to lighten up.'

Her light green eyes had sparkled, shining with amusement.

But this was why he had wanted her to leave, this cell and her inert body, drained of precious blood, his greatest fear made manifest, that a woman, any woman, would die because of him, because she knew him or got too close.

*** *** ***

Abigail thought she was breathing but she couldn't be sure. Did it count as breathing if you sort of puffed your air in and out of your chest? Her ribs hurt. To draw a deep breath hurt too much and yet that wasn't the real problem. The truth was, she didn't have the strength to draw a deep breath and her blood felt heavy again, her heart sluggish. Gerrod must be close and in need.

Gerrod, she called out, pathing along his particular frequency. *I'm here.*

Where is here?

In an Invictus prison.

Huh. A prison? They're that organized?

It's a new terrible night for Merhaine.

I'm so sorry. She had another question, but it just wasn't coming to the front of her mind. What was it that she needed to know? In fact, she'd been feeling quite desperate to have this particular question answered.

Finally she found it. *Are you dead?*

Okay that came out wrong, but it was close to the question she wanted to ask.

Did she hear him chuckle?

No, I'm not dead. Close, though.

Oh. She felt too weak to be sad. Another question worked in her mind. *Is there any way out of this mess?*

Not sure. I can't move.

Are you behind me?

Yes.

She rolled…sort of. More like scraping and pushing with a hand then her knee, maybe a foot. It was so hard to move and her ribs hurt like hell. Finally, she turned over onto her right side, but had to pant through a few more short breaths. Even then, she couldn't see Gerrod. She couldn't see anything. There was some kind of veil over her eyes.

With great difficulty, she lifted her hand and pushed the veil away, which turned out to be a wall made up of her hair.

Gerrod came into focus, sitting not five feet from her, and she smiled.

He was so handsome even though he looked like a bowl of cupcake flour right now, perfectly white. She chuckled, or thought she did, because he actually looked like a vampire. Gone was all that deep rich skin tone.

Okay, now she felt sad.

Gerrod. I don't want this to be the end. We were just figuring things out.

He pathed, but a different language rippled through her mind. *English*, she murmured along that same amazing telepathic lane she'd learned to cruise so recently.

Chapter Seven

Gerrod closed his eyes. Looking at her felt like sharp glass cutting into his heart. She was right. They had just started figuring things out, like what a human was doing in his world, setting up a bakery in his lands, having the power to reach his personal frequency, why sex between them was earth-shattering.

But maybe the biggest question was why had he held back from her, resisted her so hard? Because in this moment nothing seemed more important than Abigail, this woman who had told him to 'lighten up', made him laugh, then took him to bed after the attack at the wedding when his heart was laden with all the unsolvable problems of his realm.

What a surprise she had been from the beginning. He had tried to get rid of her, for several reasons. Although this had been the main one, that she hadn't been safe in his world.

Was this really to be the end? What would become of his people? Was it possible the Invictus were poised to dominate all the Nine North American Realms?

He opened his eyes once more. Abigail rested her head on her arm, breaths still shallow, eyes shut.

What came to him seemed to arrive on a golden stream of light, flooding his mind and helping him to understand the true state of his heart: Even if he should survive this moment, if Abigail perished, what joy would he ever know again? She had become this great, brilliant sun in his life, shining on everything, brightening the dullest shadow, giving ease to his heart, and great pleasure to his body. Even her blood had a special quality that…

The thought splintered and a new one was born.

Her blood.

Abigail's blood. Her 'blood rose' blood. He had forgotten the unique properties of her blood, that it was impervious to wraith blood.

A plan began to form in his mind, a great deception.

Abigail, he sent.

Hunh? Barely there.

Would you do me the honor of becoming my blood rose?

A long, long pause.

Finally, *Are you sure that's what you want?*

Yes. I think there is a mystery here and I intend to embrace it.

Her eyes fluttered open. He tilted his head to see her expression better. Was there a smile on her pale lips?

Would you be able to live if I agreed to become your blood rose?
I think so.

Then of course I'll agree. But just so ya know, I was coming back, Gerrod. I had already made the decision to come back to Merhaine.

Just like that, it was settled between them, in a dank Invictus prison. Dear Goddess, just like that.

He shook his head. He understood then the greatest part of who she was and why he loved her as much as he did: She would always sacrifice herself for those she loved.

"Wraith," he called out, but his voice was hardly more than a whisper. He took several deep breaths. "Wraith." Stronger this time.

The wraith appeared, her red flowing gown moving about as though having a life of its own. Wraiths were always in flight and almost always barefoot. "Did you have something you wished to say, Mastyr of Merhaine?"

"I wish to complete the Invictus coupling you suggested to me earlier, with the human. I will not have her die because I am being stubborn."

Gerrod?

Trust me.

The wraith's eyes, all that silver, opened wide. "My mastyr will be pleased. Of course it is very experimental, but we have had profound results. One day, we will prevail." And there it was, the truth of all this organization. A mastyr vampire had taken the Invictus in hand and now worked to build a force against all the realms.

"Don't delay," Gerrod said. "She will not live much longer."

Her gaze lowered to Abigail. "The human is very weak but the coupling will heal her."

She sped away, her robes flapping behind like great red wings.

Gerrod, are we to become Invictus?

Trust...me. His vision grew dark and as he slid down the wall, he hoped to hell the wraith took him at his word.

Embrace the Dark

** *** ***

Abigail felt arms pick her up. She glanced to her left. The vampire who had taken her blood, probably joined to the wraith now hovering nearby, held her steady. She whimpered because of her ribs.

"You will grow stronger, never fear," the wraith said, floating in front of Abigail. "Then you'll see the true majesty of what we intend to accomplish in the realm world."

A troll slave shuffled toward her. She bore a silver chain, threaded through iron rings that dangled from each ear. The chain was caught below her chin and clamped together and travelled inside her beige muslin shirt. Abigail didn't want to know where it ended. The slave waited beside the wraith, her head tipped submissively down, or maybe it was the weight of the chain dragging down her ears.

"Slave, you will take the knife and open the human's vein."

The troll stepped close to Abigail, took her arm in her hand, then cut her wrist open, a deep wound that made Abigail cry out. She opened her eyes and saw that the wraith held a bowl beneath her arm. She watched what little blood she had left stream into the pure white vessel.

"Good. That will do." The raspy voice of the wraith flowed down from above her.

The troll bound her arm with gauze as Abigail looked around. Gerrod lay on the floor on his side. He looked horribly still.

She gasped. *Gerrod?* she pathed.

But nothing returned, just a blank emptiness. She turned and looked up at the wraith. "Is he dead?"

"No. Close. But this should work."

"He won't be able to drink."

The wraith smiled, her yellow fangs so strange against her dark lips. "He won't need to drink," the wraith said. "We have many methods for completing the symbiotic bond."

A chill traveled over Abigail's neck. What did she mean?

The troll moved to Gerrod and bunched his sleeve above his elbow. She then cut him deep, not at the wrist but high on his forearm. Blood pumped slowly into the bowl, as in way-too-slow, rhythmic spurts, which was the only sign Abigail had that his heart still beat. After no more than fifteen seconds, the troll slapped a bandage on the wound. She returned the bowl to the wraith.

The wraith snapped her fingers at the troll then laughed as she extended her arm down to the slave. She levitated lower so that the troll could reach her wrist. "Make the cut, but not too severe, or the next cut will be on you."

The troll trembled as she whipped the knife over the wraith's veins at the wrist. The wraith didn't even flinch. She let a good portion drip into the bowl.

When she was done, the troll bandaged her wrist.

The wraith then used what looked like a single chop stick to swirl the blood together. She breathed in deeply, her thin nostrils flaring. Her very white cheeks colored up and her fangs seemed to press down on her lower lip.

"The bouquet. Like bread dipped in wine. Exquisite."

Abigail still panted each breath, waiting.

The wraith's fangs retreated. She called out over her shoulder. "Bring me the syringe. We must do this now. He no longer breathes."

Abigail drew in a sharp painful breath. She glanced at Gerrod's chest and sides. The wraith was right. "Hurry."

The slave helped the wraith fill the syringe with half the combined blood. With her foot, she pushed Gerrod onto his back.

"Expose his chest."

The troll dropped to her knees and used the knife to cut through the shoulder strap. She made quick cuts at both front panels of the leather coat at the shoulders then sliced up his woven shirt. Within seconds, he was stripped to the waist, his heavily muscled pecs and strong abs horribly white under the glare of the fluorescent lights.

There was nothing pretty about this moment, just horror and pain.

"Step away," the wraith commanded.

The slave rose and moved backward in quick short steps.

The wraith dropped to her knees, her hair still wafting back and forth. She put one hand on Gerrod's chest and felt the spacing between the ribs.

Before Abigail could take the next breath, she slammed the syringe down into Gerrod's body. This alone caused him to jerk, which gave Abigail some hope that he wasn't too far gone. She depressed the plunger and the combined blood flowed into his heart.

He began to twitch.

She couldn't take her eyes off him, not even when the wraith moved close and put the bowl to Abigail's lips. She watched Gerrod as she drank the rest of their combined blood.

One second.

Two.

Three.

Gerrod's skin color returned but soon ran an almost fiery red.

But that was the last she saw, because Abigail threw her head back and screamed. The pain was almost unbearable. Between her ribs and what the combined blood was doing to her, now she really couldn't breathe. She just stared up at the ugly box light fixture, panting once more in light breaths. She felt as though her blood was doing battle with the wraith's blood. Maybe it was.

The pain pulsed through her, driving into her head, setting every joint aching like she was being pummeled. Her skin felt blistered with heat.

But even through all this pain, for a moment, her mind seized, and her life began to roll before her, of the tragic deaths of her parents, the frequent and at times constant illness her sister endured, Abigail working nights and weekends while she finished her senior year in high school, later majoring in realm studies at Northern Arizona University but never completing her degree, of opening a bakery, of her sister's health improving, then Megan's wedding and the birth of her children.

But it was first seeing Gerrod that her mind grabbed, the sheer breadth of his shoulders, the fine angle of his back to a narrow waist, the fierce power of his thighs, the frequent look on his face when he would turn and stare at her, his expression so angry, as though she'd intruded on his life in order to torment him. Yet, how well she knew him now, that all that anger was a mask of deep concern for his people, the weight he bore in his soul, even his attraction to her, all that pulled his brow low and gave him a constant scowling appearance.

As the visions stopped, she realized her pain was gone and in its place was a thumping heartbeat, stronger than she'd ever known. She glanced at the wraith and something nagged at her, something that she had heard two weeks ago about wraith blood.

Enlightenment dawned as she remembered what Vojalie had said about a blood rose being impervious to wraith blood. She stared at Gerrod. He must have remembered this as well, which was why he knew neither could become the heinous symbiotic pair that enjoyed killing.

She focused within her body and felt it, her blood overcoming the wraith infection.

She sat up.

She stared at the wraith whose silver eyes glowed with a mad light. "You are now Invictus."

Like hell I am, she thought. But all she did was dip her chin then turn to stare at Gerrod.

Her vision seemed changed, as though he had an aura around him. That aura drew her.

She rose to her feet in a fluid motion, her body completely healed. She felt better than she had ever felt in her life, except for the weight of the excess blood she had made for Gerrod. Yep, she was ready for her vampire again.

But now it all made sense, what at least one of her purposes in Gerrod's life would be, now and forever. She crossed to him and dropped to stretch down beside him. She laid a hand on his chest.

He was breathing much better now, but the redness of his skin had faded and he was now once again very pale. She knew the cause: chronic blood starvation. Even the power latent in their combined bloods could not suddenly restore this amount of deprivation. Although as a blood rose, she'd had the opposite experience.

She touched his face. *Drink from me*, she said, mind-to-mind.

He blinked slowly, as though he wasn't fully able to comprehend his surroundings.

Take from me all that you need and grow powerful once more.

He blinked again and his vision cleared. He dragged in a breath and his nostrils flared.

He fell on her, attacking her neck, sinking his fangs. He started to drink.

In the distance, she heard the wraith's approval.

She slid her hands up into his long, thick hair and savored the feel of him taking her blood that he might live. Her body grew alive beneath his, straining against him as her hands slid over his bare muscled back.

As her heart evened out, she sighed. She understood now that the more she had been around Gerrod, the more blood she had produced, as though her body had understood on a hormonal level, even from the beginning, what she was long before Vojalie had spoken the words: *blood rose*.

*** *** ***

Gerrod felt born anew. Abigail's blood had returned his life to him. At the same time, he could feel a waning battle in his blood stream: the taint of wraith blood against the antidote of a blood rose. A few seconds more, and a stream of peace flowed through him. His blood was now pure. Abigail had prevailed.

His body pounded with life and he was fully aroused against her, but his mind was alive with the other truth, that he had a ruse to continue until he could get his woman to safety.

He shifted his mind to focus on anything but the warm soft

body beneath all his hardness of muscle and desire.

He thought of Abigail's bakery and the unimportant cupcakes that had brought the most important thing into his life.

He had Gus to thank for Abigail's presence in his life, Gus of the pink and purple embroidered socks, who never feared to call him on the carpet for his bad behavior, Gus, who's sweet tooth had taken him into Flagstaff one fateful day, and to a bakery called *Just too Sweet!*, which led to a second bakery, *Just Two Sweet!*

Which led him here.

And safe to rise from her.

He stood up and extended his hand down. Her eyes glowed, just as they would were they both Invictus now. How strange to think the same coupling that created the perversion known as Invictus, also created the bond between a blood rose and a mastyr vampire.

She took his hand and he lifted her easily to her feet.

The show must continue, so he pulled her into his arms and kissed her hard, forcefully, pushing her head back until she slumped against him.

"So the bond is complete," the wraith said.

Gerrod looked at the wraith who was now cast in a luminous glow. It took a moment for Gerrod to realize that he was seeing the wraith through new eyes, the bonded powerful eyes of a vampire and his rose.

"Tell me who is your leader? To whom do I owe the privilege of service now?"

The wraith actually smiled. "Neither the Great Mastyr nor his mistress are here and for now, you do not need to know more. But my mastyr did wish me to welcome you both to the fold."

There was a woman.

The netting that trapped him was soaked in a magic oil that blocked his powers.

The Great Mastyr was bonded with a powerful fae.

Understanding flowed, why there had been so many more attacks and how he had been trapped in a net. The Invictus now had a powerful leader and perhaps even an equally powerful faery driving this renewed attack of the Invictus.

He would ponder all this later, share his information with the other mastyr vampires, and of course with Vojalie who was the acknowledged leader of the powerful fae of North America.

For now, he had a compound to escape with Abigail by his side.

Gerrod glanced down and saw that his clothes were ruined. There was nothing to be done, but continue the ruse wearing only his leathers and his boots.

He squared his shoulders as he held Abigail's hand and walked from the cell. He felt within himself a power he had never before experienced, that which the bond to Abigail had given him. He felt his war frequency and knew the power lay therein.

He didn't open it because he felt certain that doing so would take the building down. Innocent slaves lived here, not just wraiths. *Abigail, prepare yourself.*

I have pathed your war frequency. I know what is coming.

He glanced at her and smiled. *Why am I not surprised?*

Yes, her eyes were still glowing. They were one, as the Invictus were one. He could understand now how the pairs were able to function in perfect unison.

I am keeping my thoughts quiet, she pathed. *Just move forward and I'll read or sense what you intend to do next. I'm with you.*

She was with him.

Extraordinary.

He was not alone.

Never again so long as she lived.

So what came to him was the absolute necessity that she live, that whatever decisions he made from this point forward, Abigail must survive.

He squeezed her hand.

He walked with her up the long hall and into the dark of night. He pathed to Derek, *How close are you? Abigail and I are leaving the compound doors. Can you see us?*

Yes. Wraiths are circling overhead. Several vampires and other realm-folk bonded to the wraiths have emerged and are now levitating as well.

Those in the air are all Invictus, but I see many slaves about.

What do you want us to do?

Retreat a distance of two hundred yards. What must happen next, I'll accomplish alone.

One of the wraiths shrieked. "Look. The enemy is departing, fleeing." A long stream of laughter followed.

He felt for his personal telepathy. Even though he knew Abigail tracked his thoughts, he pathed, *Ready?*

Yes.

He closed his eyes and as he extended his left arm, summoning his war power, she slung an arm around his neck and planted her foot on the top of his heavy boot.

He looked up into the sky and saw that a dozen wraiths circled in an excited state.

Slaves huddled near the walls of the building.

His power began to rise.

He heard violent shrieking all above him, where wraiths and the wraith-bonded realm-folk circled. The enemy finally understood, but it was too late.

He released his power and it was like a red wall of fire that rolled upward in the direction of the levitating Invictus. Within a split second, the monsters were on fire and raced in every direction through the air trying to stop the burning, but the flames only grew brighter and higher.

He smelled charred flesh and heard the sounds of death groans. He set his body in flight, just a foot off the ground and sped his way north faster than ever before. Within seconds he reached Derek, who hovered above the trees.

"You will escort us back to the castle at which time we will make plans. Follow me. I'm taking Abigail home."

Derek gave a brisk nod and called out the orders.

Gerrod adjusted his arm around Abigail, savoring her warm soft body pressed against his. He held her tight.

He turned and once more set his tremendous speed on a path to the castle.

As Derek, Jason and the rest of the Guard, as well as their attending forces, gathered in levitated flight behind him, flying in a solid V formation, Gerrod smiled.

Mastyr Vampire Gerrod, Mastyr of Merhaine, smiled.

He felt fingers on his lips.

You're smiling, Abigail pathed.

Yes. I am.

Embrace the Dark

*** *** ***

Abigail was changed.

She stood in Gerrod's library, at the top of the table, her fingertips touching the dark polished oak. Her gaze was fixed to him as he spoke with Derek and Jason. He was sending them on the much needed rescue mission.

She could feel her frequencies developing within her so fast that it amazed her. Vojalie had said she would become vampire, and so that change was underway as well, while Gerrod spoke to his men and orchestrated the next step in the battle against the enemy.

"The acreage near the compound has become verdant farmland. I saw many workers. Slaves, no doubt."

"Our realm-folk?"

"Undoubtedly. I know that as I released the war frequency, at least a dozen Invictus couples were destroyed. There might, however, be more in the compound. I'm not sure. Take the Guardsmen and finish what I began."

Jason smiled. "With pleasure."

The men left the library, walked quickly through the great entrance hall, and began calling their troops together.

She followed Gerrod to the front lawn and watched the score of powerful men launch, flying fast in that strange foot-above-the-ground levitation that many realm-folk could master in time.

He took hold of her hand and for a long time she stood with him in the open night air, taking a moment, a breath, to just be.

She had come home to Merhaine, no longer just human, but more. *Vampire.*

"Are you okay?" He asked.

She nodded, squeezing his hand. "Changing," she said.

He turned her toward her. "How are your gums?"

"Sore. How do I release the fangs?"

He smiled softly and kissed her lips. "It will just feel right then you'll release them."

She sighed. "This is all so strange. My body feels like a cauldron of weighted sensations, of change, of frequencies forming."

Did he just growl?

"What was that?" she asked laughing.

"You'll have your own frequency now, your own personal waves of energy."

"Oh," she murmured, her brows rising high on her forehead. This had possibilities. "You mean, like the frequency you have? The one that pounds on me?"

He nodded.

She lowered her gaze from his then focused internally, on the various frequencies crowding her body. She searched through them, as though picking each up by the hand then releasing them.

Finding the frequency that called her mate, was like touching something electric. She looked up at him, and as though understanding all at once, she opened the waves of energy and let them flow.

Gerrod took a step back and put a fist to his chest. "By the Goddess's pink nipples…"

He recovered swiftly and with his chin lowered, he took her in his arms and kissed her. Because her frequency was open, and he suddenly pounded her with his frequency, she shrieked and backed up. Her eyes rolled in her head as all this sensation flowed over her body in lightening waves. She was instantly close to an orgasm.

He caught her and kept her from falling, and gathered her in his arms once more.

That was when her fangs slipped through her gums and were suddenly just there.

She stared at his neck. She wanted to bite him.

But because her connection to him was so profound, she also felt that Jason was contacting him telepathically. He stared down at her his eyes wide, dilated, his body trembling. "I need to take you to bed."

"Or throw me across this table."

His eyes fluttered.

Jason's path rang louder this time.

"Hold that thought," he said.

He opened the pathway and she heard Jason's voice as clearly in her mind as it was no doubt speeding through his. *The Invictus are toast, to the last symbiotic pair. We're burning what's left of them now. Derek has our realm-folk in hand. All alive. Much weeping and giving of thanks to the Goddess. At least a hundred had been enslaved to serve this, I don't know what, tribe maybe?*

Gerrod's voice rang through her mind as he pathed, *See that everyone is returned home tonight.*

My thoughts as well. When we're done, do you want us back at the castle?

Only those Guardsmen on scheduled duty need return here. But tomorrow night, please have the entire Guard come to the training compound. We'll talk then. Let everyone rest.

Derek and his team will be patrolling the wastelands until

..ank you, Jason

See you tomorrow, mastyr.

*** *** ***

Gerrod shut his telepathic pathway down, hopefully for the rest of the night.

He had other critical business to attend to and held all that business in his arms, his gaze fixed on the sharp points of Abigail's fangs. The human was now vampire, his woman, his blood rose, his savior.

He leaned down and ran his tongue over her lips, over the upper portions of her fangs, felt her mouth open for him, and he thrust deep, avoiding the razor points. He pulled her tight against him, wanting her to feel all that he was as a man, all that he wanted her to have, all that he needed to give her.

And he wanted to travel down her frequency, taste of her waves over and over. "I need you in my bed."

She smiled.

He slid his arm behind her knees and picked her up, carrying her back into the castle.

Gus waited at the threshold, dancing from foot to foot. "Mastyr?" he inquired. "What is the news?"

Gerrod smiled. "Jason and the Guard have rescued all the missing realm-folk. The Invictus, at our wastelands, are dead."

"Thank the merciful Goddess." His gaze shifted to Abigail. "And will the Mistress be staying with us?"

Gerrod turned to Abigail then leaned down and kissed her. "I have it on excellent authority she never plans on leaving Merhaine again, except to visit her family, of course."

Abigail smiled.

"Oh, blessed night, most blessed night." Augustus continued in this theme, but Gerrod moved past him and carried his prize deep into the castle, down the long hall to his private suite. He slammed the door shut with his foot, turned, and locked the damn thing. Ethan would have been proud of him.

He wasn't exactly sure when he would emerge, or when he would next let the castle staff see Abigail, but the rest of the night was his.

He carried her through the bedroom and into the bathroom. He didn't set her down until he had her near the shower. He turned the water on, glancing at her over his shoulder. She was staring up at the ceiling touching her new fangs, then wincing when she punctured her thumb. "Wow, they're sharp."

A growl left his throat unbidden.

She blinked at him and smiled.

"You look so pretty with those fangs."

She turned and moved to the sink to look at herself in the mirror. "How do I get rid of them?"

"Don't. Not yet. You'll need them and I want them."

She rolled her eyes at him. "I just want to practice."

He unbuckled his boots and removed them.

"So what do I do?" she asked, still prodding her gums.

"It is sometimes helpful to merely focus carefully on what it is you want to do." She turned toward him ready to ask another question, but at that moment he slid his leathers down his thighs so that now he was fully exposed and aroused.

She blinked several times, her gaze low. Her tongue made an

_ou are so wicked. But I want to get the hang of this."

_inished removing his pants and smiled. "Then by all _ans, you should practice."

He hopped in the shower and soaped up. He scrubbed hard, wanting to get clean of his captivity. He had just finished washing his hair, when he felt her near. Then her hands were on him and she was stroking his pecs, running her fingers the breadth of his chest.

For just this moment, a vibration passed through him that had nothing to do with either of their frequencies. He felt as though the universe had just shifted position, making an adjustment long needed, and suddenly the world was right, entirely right, wholly right.

When she put her arms around him and laid her head against his chest, and his arms found and held her, he knew the adjustment had been made, finalized, perfected. He was home.

But there was one last piece of this puzzle, that which Vojalie had warned them was necessary to complete the final bonding to his blood rose so that every other mastyr vampire would know she belonged just to him.

An exchange of frequencies while mating.

Like hell he could tolerate any other mastyr vampire getting within a yard of her until she was well and truly his.

"I want to wash my hair," she said kissing his chest, then looking up at him.

"Allow me."

He took his time and washed it for her, lathering up all that glorious long red length. This was how everything had begun just a couple of weeks ago, in the shower, hair shampooed, rinse applied.

But this time, he was caring for her hair.

He added the crème rinse and took a moment to turn her toward him, to fondle her breasts, her stomach, the soft flesh between her legs, until he buried two fingers inside her. He kissed her deeply, her fangs now receded to safety, so that he could plunge his tongue into her.

I love you, he pathed.

An odd sound like, mnmhmnnn, came out of her.

He drew back and smiled.

"Ah, that half-smile of yours." She kissed both sides of his mouth then looked up to meet his gaze. "I love you, too, more than I can say."

"Let's rinse your hair so I can take you to bed."

A few minutes later, he carried her into his bedroom.

*** *** ***

Abigail lay in the middle of Gerrod's bed, her bed now, staring up into the eyes of the vampire she had come to love. She still couldn't believe that this had happened to her, not just that she was now vampire, but that love had found her.

He leaned down and kissed her, his lips soft, moist, sensual. His frequency was open and pummeling her all over, very low right now. They were just getting started. He had his car on idle and even in this state it was pure heaven.

She smoothed her hand over his cheek, just savoring him, the look of him, feel and smell of him. It was like being surrounded by mountains and oceans and everything big on the earth.

He was propped up on his arms, holding himself above her, his knees between her legs, his rigid cock stroking her abdomen onderful promise.

is more than I ever expected to know in my entire life," .uid.

His head dipped and his smile emerged again. He kissed her hard, pushing his tongue into her mouth. After a long moment, he drew back. "Words cannot express all that I feel. I am overwhelmed one moment to the next. I will ask only this: What can I do for you? Tell me what can I do."

"Well," she drawled. "My blood is a bit lumpish. How about you start by taking care of that?"

He groaned. His lower hardness shifted and began pushing against what was ready for him. He kissed her again. *I can't believe that what I need is here, with me.*

It's my pleasure, she returned. *Giving you what you need has been one of the greatest joys of my life.*

Abigail, you please me in endless ways. Thank you for coming back to Merhaine. You have made my life complete.

He shifted slightly, drifting his lips over her cheek to glide down her neck. He begin licking the skin above her vein. He was thrusting steadily now, pushing in, pulling back. Her heart beat fast now, readying for him.

Take all you need, she pathed.

He struck. The jab stunned her as he opened the vein, then pulled out. But the moment he began to suck, and draw her blood into his mouth, her body fell into the most delicious lethargy. Pleasure began building and his vibration came stronger now. He groaned and was breathing hard.

So good. Oh, Abigail, I've been starved for so long. You are a banquet.

Tears slipped from her eyes. She surrounded him with her arms, caressing the muscles of his shoulders, arms and back. His rhythm, as he stroked and sucked, filled her with deepening pleasure. She savored those sensual waves of energy, which he released at every point of his body, his fingers, his chest, and his cock deep within. Yes, the vibrations were *aaaaahhhh*.

She moaned softly. *Gerrod, I love that you're taking my blood. Like fire in my body.*

He finished drinking but sustained his rhythm. He looked down at her. "I know I have blood on my mouth."

"I know, now kiss me."

He crashed down on her, kissing her hard. She cried out against his mouth, overcome with the swell of emotion that kept riding her chest. *So much pleasure.*

Will you take my blood now?

When he drew back, she asked, "How?"

He smiled and his hips grew still. In a smooth turn, as though he was simply moving her through water, he rolled and brought her on top of him, still connected low.

Her head was dizzy from the unexpected movement, but she smiled. "You always surprise me."

"Good." His hips flexed and because the position had changed, she felt him inside her in an entirely new way. "Oh, Gerrod."

He didn't say anything but exposed his neck.

A shiver passed through her that heightened all the waves of energy still playing over her. The part of her that was newly vampire looked at the contour of the exposed skin, the angle of the jaw, the shape of the ear, the placement of the clavicle. It was as though she could measure every millimeter from one point to

..'t try to analyze her next move, but rather went with ..incts. As she lowered to lick a long line up his throat, she re..lized some new part of her was actually *hungry*. And there it was, her first understanding of blood hunger.

She licked his throat several times, pulling back each time to watch his neck shift and the vein rise. A swell of desire propelled her forward, her fangs emerged, and she sunk them. She felt Gerrod's hips jerk and his vibration seemed to get stronger. Oh, God, all these sensations. The fangs retreated and blood flowed. She formed a seal around the skin and suckled.

But as she did, her hips began a serious pistoning motion as though driven by her blood-need. The taste was not what she expected, but rather flavored like his scent, like fresh rain, which seemed so impossible and yet was like everything she knew Gerrod to be.

When his blood reached her stomach, the fireworks began, little sparks dancing everywhere, even in her veins. She moaned. His hands were on her hips now and he took over the thrusting, his muscled thighs pumping her hard, the rippling waves of energy taking her to the edge.

She was so close.

I'm close.

Just let go.

Two more sucks and the orgasm gripped her, rolling along all her sensitive flesh and flying up through her body, up and up until she released his neck, arched away from him, and the final sensation crested. She screamed and writhed, savoring the ecstasy, the deep fulfillment, the intensity of his energy moving in powerful waves, over her and through her. And the whole time, he thrust up into her, helping all that pleasure to go on and on.

At last, she stilled above him, arms stretched out, eyes closed. He took both her hands in his. "Look at me."

She couldn't quite focus but she eased back toward him and planted her hands on either side of him. She met his piercing blue eyes and fell into them. He flexed his hips. He was still very hard within her.

"Abigail, release your frequency for me."

"This will complete our bond, won't it?" She knew she held within her similar waves of energy. She just wasn't sure she could survive another blissful experience.

But his smile appeared and his eyelids fell to half-mast. "According to Vojalie it will and it is most necessary. I want all my brethren mastyr vampires to be warned away from you. After what I experienced with Ethan that night at the bakery, I am convinced only a bond will serve."

"Then I'd better find my frequency right now."

She drew in a small breath and began searching deep within. At the same time, she rocked her hips, pushing against his thrusts, gripping him down low in a way that had his neck arching.

"Sweet Goddess," he whispered.

As her own pleasure began to build all over again, as his blood streaked through her veins, setting her on fire once more, she hunted through her emerging frequencies. So many pathways to learn and to explore, but this one was a gift she could give to Gerrod. The continuous stroking of his own energy against her body was as though fingers touched and fondled her everywhere. She wanted that for him in return.

She found the pathway and smiled down at him. She began to release her energy. When she did, the pleasure she felt doubled, that was the only way she could explain it. She was close all over again.

Gerrod looked up at her, his brow creased, but only because he was damn close. He groaned.

"Yes," she whispered. She leaned down and kissed him. He was so hard inside her.

"Your vibration, *dear Goddess*."

"Yes."

His hips began moving faster, until all she did was hold herself steady and look at him. The pulsing of his energy grew stronger, which ignited her own.

Then suddenly, the two vibrations touched and began to pass through each other. She felt drawn toward his body at the same time, and stretched out on top of him, needing to be close. She was panting and his breaths matched her own. His eyes had a wild look now.

"Gerrod."

He reached up toward her . "Abigail." She leaned down, putting her mouth on his. He thrust his tongue inside. The sensation kept rolling as Gerrod drove into her. She was trembling now as he wrapped his powerful arms around her.

I'm ready, she pathed.

Good. Do you feel that?

Like the rumbling of a train. Oh…God.

The explosion of ecstasy was abrupt and profound, as though the orgasm took hold of her entire body and his, as though she could feel his and he could feel hers.

The kiss broke, and he shouted into the ceiling, words of a different language as he came. But his voice sounded a million miles away. Her head felt full of a rushing wind, and pleasure kept flowing up her body and back, waves and more waves.

"Oh, my God," she cried.

Gerrod continued to thrust, so long as the shared frequencies flowed. Finally, each frequency retreated and pulled apart, leaving a beautiful lethargy behind. She relaxed against him, tucking her head beneath his chin. Her eyes closed.

She breathed in and out, savoring the rise and fall of his chest, the strength of his arms, that she was still connected with him, still one with him.

After a moment, she rose up to look at him. Somehow, it seemed very important. He opened his eyes and smiled, his wonderful half-smile.

"Hey," she whispered. She touched his lips with her fingers. "That was amazing."

"I didn't know it could be like that." He pushed her damp hair behind her ears. "You're beautiful Abigail."

She smiled. "I love you."

"And I love you." His deep warm voice rolled over her.

Without warning, the bond tightened. She gasped. "Do you feel that?"

His eyes widened. He put a hand first to his chest then to hers. "It's as though an invisible cord stretches between us."

"Exactly and when you said you loved me, it tightened."

"Yes, that is exactly what it felt like."

"So we're officially bonded, mastyr vampire and blood rose."

At that, he released a deep breath and smiled. "I just can't believe it, though." He stroked the side of her neck. "And you truly feel better and not at all weak?"

"Better, absolutely. When you have need of blood, my body gets busy producing what you need."

His arms tightened around her. "Then I start producing what you need."

Since she could feel him low and that he was aroused once more, her whole body arched with desire. "It seems like a really fair exchange." She smiled then laughed.

"I love your laugh. Have I told you that?"

"No. In fact, there was a time not too long ago when you complained of my laughter."

He grew somber, his expression more serious. "I wanted you so much, I couldn't do anything but stay close to you and be irritable. Now here you are and all is changed."

"Everything has changed. I spoke with Megan. She encouraged me to come back. I think she knew I was in love with you all that time."

"She is a good woman."

"The best."

He leaned up and kissed her, then in that fast, fluid-like movement of his, but completely without warning, he flipped her over on the bed so that now he was on top. Before she could complain about the suddenness of the move, however, he was thrusting inside her once more.

*** *** ***

Abigail stared up at Vojalie's ceiling. "I find it enchanting. Is it fae magic that makes it move?" She glanced back at Vojalie.

Davido had once again taken Gerrod back into his pride-and-joy vegetable garden so that the women could talk.

The lovely fae woman sat on the sofa, looking up as well. "No. It always reflects the inhabitants of the room. You're seeing your own sense of wonder."

Abigail smiled. "I have felt this way from the moment I first entered Merhaine over a year ago, full of wonder, enchantment maybe."

"Merhaine agrees with you as does being vampire. You took his blood?"

She turned toward Vojalie and crossed the room to sit opposite her on the left facing sofa just as she had done a couple of weeks ago. "I did."

"And?"

Abigail marveled that she wasn't embarrassed. "It was as though I had come home, as though I had been looking for Gerrod my entire life, always carrying a profound longing in my heart. Taking his blood was like planting my feet in his room, staking my claim. I told him I would never leave. I belong here."

"Yes, you do." She pressed her stomach then drew in a breath. "Sometimes the baby likes to stretch out. At this stage, never a good thing." But she smiled and there was a tenderness in her eyes. "Do you want to have children?"

The question surprised Abigail, since she had never really stopped her life long enough to think about being a mother, but what was the answer?

She pondered the idea of being in a forever kind of relationship with Gerrod, like Megan and Joe. She loved her niece and nephew. But now she understood why she had never considered having a family of her own. She had been waiting for this day, when the right man would come to her.

She smiled. "I didn't think so. But with Gerrod, everything feels possible."

"That is such a beautiful answer. Did you hear that, Gerrod?"

Abigail should have known he was behind her and now that Vojalie had spoken his name, she could feel him. The bond they shared tightened and spread pleasure through her chest and deep into her heart.

As she turned and saw him, she put a hand to her breast and her eyes filled with tears. Gerrod was so beautiful and he was smiling, just off to the side of his mouth. His eyes were glowing as well. So much affection, so much love.

She moved without thinking and rose to cross to him. He opened his arms and she landed within, her head pressed to his chest. There was no more hesitation from him as had happened several times before she had returned to Merhaine. His arms engulfed her and held her tight.

She closed her eyes and two fat tears trickled down her cheeks. She squeezed as hard as she could.

I love you, Abigail.

No response seemed adequate. To say she simply 'loved' him seemed so much less than she felt. Finally, she spoke aloud. "You fill my heart with such joy. You have no idea."

She felt Vojalie nearby. "When you are ready, we will have the evening meal on the patio. For now, stay in this room as long as you like, but don't forget to look up."

Vojalie and her husband headed toward the hall.

"We could offer them the guest room for an hour or two,"

Davido said.

"Oh, don't be so crass," Vojalie whispered.

"How about instead I take you to our room for an hour or two?"

"Have you noticed how pregnant I am?"

"When did that ever stop us?"

"Will you please stop pinching me." Giggles followed then faded as the couple disappeared down the hall.

Abigail shifted slightly in Gerrod's arms so that she could look up at him. His lips found hers in a slow tender kiss.

When he pulled back, he said, "You would have children with me?"

"I think so. A dozen if you like. But not all at once."

He shook his head. "I never thought to have this. My life was so complicated and now it seems so simple."

"Me, too. I thought I knew what my life was, then you kissed me in the forest."

"And you told me to lighten up."

"I just wanted to see your smile."

He thumbed her cheek and kissed her once more. "I love you."

"And I love you so much it hurts."

His smile again.

Movement above caught her eye. She remembered Vojalie's words so she glanced up at the ceiling. She drew in a sharp breath. "Gerrod, look."

The ceiling was alive and glowing, moving in iridescent shades of blue and light green with occasional lightning streaks of red flashing through. "So beautiful. Vojalie said the ceiling reflects the inhabitants of the room. This must be you and me, what we are together, right this moment."

He turned her in his arms so that she was supported with her back against his chest. "At the very least, that's what this feels like. Only I think what I feel is a thousand times brighter than this reflection."

"At least a thousand times." She squeezed his arms.

She remained with him for some time, looking up, feeling the affection of his embrace. He rocked her slowly, side-to-side, a dance of love. She had entered his world to open a bakery, of all things, and instead had fallen in love with a vampire who ruled an entire realm.

There would be difficulties ahead, but she wouldn't think about that now, only that Gerrod held her engulfed in his massive arms and she belonged to him. Now and forever.

The End

About The Author

Caris Roane is the award-winning author of five published novels for St. Martin's Press and almost fifty published novels and novellas writing sweet Regency Romance as Valerie King.

The second installment of the Blood Rose Novella Series is: EMBRACE THE MAGIC and is currently scheduled as a summer 2012 release.

For more information about all things *Caris Roane*, please visit her website at:

www.CarisRoane.com

To be the first to learn about all upcoming Caris Roane releases, be sure to sign up for her newsletter!

And finally, if you enjoy *sweet* Regency Romance or sensual Regency Historicals, you can learn more about Valerie King at:

www.ValerieKing-Romance.com

18078824R00099

Made in the USA
Lexington, KY
13 October 2012